For Bob,
my other half, my biggest fan

I've always believed that the world was filled with opposites like black and white, good and evil, or sin and grace. There was right and wrong with nothing in between. I guess, growing up a preacher's daughter in a small town, that's to be expected. Life should be structured, ordered, and secure. I need these things. I have these things, at least I did until tonight, or this morning, whatever time it was when my husband shook me out of a deep sleep. Now, as I sit in my walk-in closet with a gun clasped in my hand and no idea why I'm here, I wonder if I've failed to recognize the opposite defining my life right now: truth and lies.

Jacob had been acting strange for the last several days. He seemed preoccupied, looking out of the windows at least every twenty minutes. Tonight, he reached an all-time high in peculiar behavior.

Jacob locked, unlocked, and relocked the front door several times. He positioned and repositioned the wooden pole he used as a stop for the sliding glass door. After about the third time checking every window to make sure they were locked, Jacob finally crawled into bed beside me. Tension radiated off of him, reaching out its tendrils and preventing either one of us from drifting to sleep. "Is everything alright?" I'd asked.

Jacob took a deep breath and blew it out. He reached over and pulled me next to him. I rested my head on his chest, while his arms encircled me. His heart pounded against my cheek. I wanted to feel safe like I usually did when he pulled me close like this, but something was definitely up. "Jacob?"

"Everything's fine." He kissed the top of my head. "At least I hope so."

Something seemed to be poking me from the inside, creeping all the way down my spine. He breathed deep and slow, a method he often used to calm himself. I found my own breathing speeding up. Part of me wanted to know what was bothering him. But the other part, the larger part of me, was afraid to ask. Whatever bothered Jacob had to be serious, but he said not to worry, so I tried to let it go. However, I had that uneasy feeling one gets just before the huge drop on a roller coaster. I tended to panic when life became unexpected. But I trusted Jacob, and if he said that everything was fine, I should believe him.

I'd trusted my father too until the evidence of his guilt became impossible to deny. I'd believed him when he insisted that he could never harm my mother. I'd defended him—until I couldn't. His words had seemed to possess truth, but not one word he spoke about that horrific day was honest. For that matter, I'm still not sure how much he ever told me that was true.

Jacob is nothing like my father. He has never given me any reason to doubt him. Nonetheless, as I drifted somewhere between being awake and asleep, I couldn't help but wonder if I was wrong to trust him. To trust anyone. There had to be some reason he was so obsessed with our home's security all of a sudden. Past hurts had a way of lingering and bleeding into the present, inflicting needless pain on harmless situations. That had to be the reason for my uneasiness—my past influenced my emotions. But I just couldn't shake the feeling that at any moment, my life's foundation would be ripped out from under me.

Again.

I'd thought that I wouldn't be able to sleep. But, when Jacob tried to wake me some time later, I had a hard time climbing out of it. "Katie, you have to get up," he said. Gentle but firm. Calm yet desperate.

I pried my eyes open, unable to focus on anything. The light from the ceiling fan burned my eyes and blinded me. Slowly Jacob's face became clear. His dark eyebrows pulled together, and his nearly black eyes bored into mine. "They've found me," he said as his eyes darted around the room. A half-whine, half-growl emerged from deep inside our German shepherd's gut. Rex paced back and forth in front of our bedroom door, looking at Jacob and then at the door.

My muddled brain tried to make sense out of what was happening. They've found me. Who? I had to be dreaming.

Jacob grabbed my hands and pulled me to a sitting position. "Katie, Sweetie, you have to wake up." Jacob circled to his side of the bed and extracted the 9 mm Glock 19 he had stowed in a bedside gun vault. At first, I'd refused a gun in the bedroom. Eventually, Jacob had convinced me; however, I'd never dreamed that he would actually need to retrieve it in the middle of the night. He pulled back the slide, sinking a round into the barrel and hurried to the walk-in closet.

I managed to stand and stagger to the door of the closet. It was even brighter in here. Jacob pulled out one side of his dresser, revealing an opening in the wall. I'd never noticed that the dresser was on hinges. Kneeling in front of the opening, he tugged out a backpack, unzipped it, and pulled out a box of bullets and a second magazine. He ejected the gun's magazine and placed another bullet in the vacant spot. The loud snap as he slammed the magazine home had a finality to it. He covered the distance to me in three large steps and thrust the gun into my hand.

"What are you doing? Why do I need this?"

"Here," he said as he pressed the second magazine into my empty hand. By the weight of the magazine, I could tell it was fully loaded. Rex barked thunderously. I jumped at the noise and nearly dropped everything. The dog ran to the door, barking over and over. He looked at me, urging me to let him out of the bedroom.

"Jacob, what's going on?"

Returning to the pack, Jacob said, "I'm sorry Katherine, but I can't explain now. You just need to trust me."

Katherine? Jacob never called me Katherine anymore. He pulled a revolver from the backpack and began loading it as fast as his fingers could.

"Jacob."

He tucked the gun in the waistband of his jeans and returned to me in two giant steps. "I'm sorry, Katie. You need to listen to me. If any of them gets past me, you need to take care of him. If anyone gets this far, you need to aim at the—"

"Wait. If who gets past you? What do you mean by take care of?"

Jacob pushed past me to the bedside table and rummaged through its top drawer. Before I could register what he was doing, he stood in front of me holding out my grandmother's rosary. "Here. This will help."

I clumsily balanced both gun and extra magazine in my right hand and held out my left. Jacob dropped the rosary in my hand and closed my fingers around it.

Without letting go, he said, "The men out there are dangerous. If any of them gets to you, you need to aim for the triangle." He drew the familiar upside-down triangle on his chest with his finger. "I mean it. You pull that trigger and don't stop until he stops, or your gun is empty." He kissed my forehead. "Remember, it's him or you, and I want it to be you. It has to be you."

I stared blankly past him, trying to understand what was happening. Jacob gently placed both of his hands on my face and turned it to face him. "You trust me, don't you?"

"I trust you," I murmured. "But I…I can't shoot a person." My voice sounded weak and shaky.

"Sure, you can. You have to. Lock the door behind me and then hide in the closet. If anyone gets this far you have to empty the gun on him. It's him or you. It has to be you. Promise me that it'll be you." He held my gaze for a couple more seconds then headed for the door. Rex vibrated with excitement as Jacob inched the door open. The dog burst out barking. "Promise me."

I nodded.

"I love you."

I nodded again.

Hands shaking, I locked the door and entered the closet.

And now, here I am, sitting with my back against the open space in the wall. Protecting. Protecting what? I consider setting the gun down to look, but then I hear

Jacob's voice in my head, "Never set down a loaded gun."

What's happening? Is this a dream? Please, dear God, let this be a dream. It doesn't make any sense. What do these men want? Does Jacob know? How can he? But he said that they'd found him. Why hadn't he told me that he was in danger? That I was in danger? Why does he have hidden guns and ammunition in the wall of our closet? What else do I not know about my husband? I feel betrayed. Lied to.

I can't resist it any longer. I shift my weight and pull Jacob's backpack closer. The sharp hissing as I open zipper to the outer compartment stops me. I stare at the door of the closet as if I might be discovered. Like ripping off a band aid, I jerk the zipper the rest of the way and reach in with my free hand. I feel booklets. Guilt tugs at my chest as I invade my husband's privacy. I should just remove my hand and zip up the pack. Before I can talk myself out of it, I snatch out the compartment's contents.

Passports. Three of them. I fumble one handed, opening the first passport. I stare at my husband's photo and read the name Jacob Varga. I open the second passport. The same smiling picture of Jacob looks back at me, only this one says Emilio Vasquez. My heart plummets. The third passport contains the same photo of Jacob with the name Jose Gomez. The name seems familiar, but I can't remember from where.

My head spins. What the hell is going on? I return the passports to the pack.

Shouting men and Rex's barking erupts from outside

the bedroom. My heart feels like it expands with every pounding heartbeat, compressing my lungs and making it difficult to take in a full breath. I wrap the rosary around my hand tighter and adjust my grip on the gun. Who are those men?

Who is Jacob?

I glance at the gun and think that I probably shouldn't be holding the rosary in the same hand that fires a death shot on some stranger. I place it around my neck.

Feeling lightheaded, I realize that I'm holding my breath. Just breathe and think about something else— anything other than the passports in that pack. I caress the pearl beads on the rosary around my neck. I know little about the rosary. My mother had been raised Catholic; however, much to her parents' dismay, she married a pastor of a non-denominational Christian church. The rosary had been first my grandmother's most cherished possession and then my mother's, which always aggravated my father, the reverend. He hated anything Catholic, and you can't get more Catholic than a rosary. My mother had held it in her hand when she died seven years ago. I'd intended to tuck it next to her in her coffin when the reverend wasn't looking; however, I couldn't bear the idea of letting it go. It was the only connection I had left to my mother. The fact that it would infuriate the reverend if he knew how much I now cherish the rosary only adds to its appeal.

It suddenly seems quieter outside the bedroom. I close my eyes to listen more closely. My stomach drops when I realize why. Rex is no longer barking. Several gunshots ring out followed by more shouting. The sound of crashing furniture and broken glass vibrates in my head.

I feel myself separating. It had happened once before, after the murder of my mother. I couldn't handle actually living through all of the implications of that day, so I'd escaped. I became an outsider looking at my own life instead of participating in it. Every time the weight of my reality would start to press down on me, I would tell myself that it wasn't real. Murdered mothers were in the movies, not in small town Harrison, in the office of a tiny Christian church where my father was pastor. I had to be dreaming.

Only, I wasn't then. And I'm not dreaming now.

Jacob had been the one to pull me back into my own life.

My hands shake violently. How can I possibly hit anything that I aim for? The doorknob on the bedroom door rattles. I draw my knees toward my chest, forming a base to rest my arms on. I glance down and see the white-gold crucifix shining on the end of the rosary—watching. I tuck it inside my t-shirt. I concentrate on breathing. In. Out. In. Out. My shoulders begin to relax.

I barely register the explosive sound of the door being kicked open. I'm in the zone now. Someone rummages noisily through the room, apparently looking for something. Maybe if I keep really quiet, he won't notice me. The closet door flings open.

My heart leaps into my throat. Breathe. My leg

cramps. I shift my weight as carefully as I can, accidentally bumping into the dresser. It swings on its hinges. The movement draws the man's attention. His eyes widen when he notices me sitting across the closet from him with a gun pointed at his chest. He's tall and thin with dark brown hair and golden eyes. I'm distracted for a moment by the deep cleft in his chin. The man recovers quickly, and a grin tugs at the corner of his mouth. The left side of his face is red and swollen. Blood drips from what looks like a bite on his right wrist. That a boy, Rex. The man sneers. "You and I both know you're not gonna use that thing."

I say nothing. I take another deep breath, my hands perfectly steady. It's him or you. It has to be you.

He takes a step toward me, and I squeeze. In that small space, the noise is deafening. I pull the trigger again and again until the gun clicks empty. With a practiced hand, I eject the magazine, put in the fresh one, and chamber another round.

I listen for commotion coming from outside the bedroom, but the ringing in my ears keeps me from hearing. The smell of spent ammunition and blood assaults my nose. I look at my victim. Blood spatters the white walls and trim behind him. Red covers his chest and seeps into the white carpet beneath him.

Oh my God. Oh my God. O my God! I have to get away from here. Away from him. But that will require me to step over the man I had just shot.

A policeman once told me that everyone is capable of killing another person else under the right circumstances. I hadn't believed him. I hadn't wanted to accept the fact that my father was a murderer. Once I had, I'd thought something was significantly wrong with the reverend's character. It was the only explanation I could accept. I'd firmly believed that I would never be able to take another person's life, regardless of the circumstance. And yet, here I am, staring at the proof.

I killed a man.

I'm trapped. My only means of escape lies just beyond the dead man. I'm shaking again and am not sure if I could stand if I tried.

Escape. I have to escape. Only I can't. I don't want to move from the safety of the closet—not until my hearing returns enough to hear what is going on outside this room.

I can't believe I killed him. The man was living, breathing, and smiling at me one second and then he's—not. I'd never seen anyone or anything die before. But, I had seen a dead body. My mother's dead body, her lifeless eyes staring.

Just like the man in my closet. Only this time, I'm the killer instead of the reverend. Could the ability to kill be genetic? I can't think about that now.

I try to stand, but my legs have fallen asleep. I grab the dresser for balance and slowly straighten up. I have to lean on it for support. I'm not sure if I'm weak from sitting so long in the closet or if I'm in shock, but I know that I can't walk yet.

Think of something else. Anything else.

I'm staring at the victim—my victim—frozen. My ears are still ringing, my head spinning. I tear my eyes from the man's face and look at the ceiling. Thankfully, there's no blood there, so it's safe. Out of the corner of my eye I spot a box that holds my tiny Christmas tree. I force myself to focus on the memory.

It was the first Christmas tree I'd bought after the death of my mother. I hadn't been able to bring myself to celebrate the holiday without her. I'd spent the two previous Christmas holidays working in an empty office on Christmas Eve and spending Christmas Day in my pajamas reading books or watching movies. Christmas had been my mother's favorite holiday. Without her, it wasn't Christmas.

That was before Jacob.

We'd been dating for about nine months when Christmas rolled around. I'd allowed myself to purchase a tiny Christmas tree. The eighteen-inch artificial tree sat in the middle of my small dining table in my studio apartment. The tree had come pre-decorated with miniature ornaments and lights. It didn't compare to the seven-foot artificial tree that I had grown up with, but it was something at least.

Jacob laughed at it. "Hey, be nice," I said. "There is no room for a bigger tree in my apartment."

There wasn't much room for Jacob in my apartment either. Jacob stood at about six-feet four and weighed about two-ten. His winter jacket pulled at his broad shoulders when he raised his arms as he gestured at my miniature tree. Jacob grinned widely, revealing deep dimples and straight white teeth. I loved those dimples. His curly dark hair was cropped short, revealing his slightly protruding ears. Somehow they lessened the intimidating effect that his size portrayed. I couldn't help but return the smile.

"Come with me, my dear," Jacob said. "Bundle up. It's pretty cold outside."

I shivered as we snaked between the picked-over rows of trees at the Christmas tree farm. The smell evoked feelings of a home where mothers lived and fathers weren't murderers. It was almost as if the scent should bring up pleasant memories from my own childhood, but if I allowed those to enter my thoughts, I'd have to think about the rest. It took about fifteen minutes for the two of us to find the perfect tree. It wasn't much taller than my five feet three inches. Except for one spot near the bottom of one side, the tree was full and beautiful.

As we drove to Jacob's house, I couldn't keep the tears from falling down my face. Jacob reached over and took my hand. "What's the matter?"

I looked away and brushed the tears off my cheeks. I swallowed hard. "Nothing's wrong," I said weakly. "It's just that…I've always dreamed of cutting down my own tree. I used to ask every year, but the reverend said that he was allergic." I'd never doubted the truth about this allergy before, but now I doubted everything he'd ever said. He probably lied about that too because he didn't want to traipse through the snow to find the perfect tree and then have to haul it home. Memories started to surface. I pressed them down.

Jacob was silent. Mentioning my childhood was rare, and I think it must have shocked us both. That was one of the things that I loved most about Jacob. He never pried me for information about my past. And, in turn, I never asked about his.

Later that night, as we admired the newly decorated tree, I said, "I could get used to this."

Jacob slid his arms around me from behind and pulled me close. "So could I." He kissed the top of my head. "This will be our new Christmas tradition."

I liked the sound of that—a new tradition for a new beginning. There would be no need to skip Christmas ever again. I laced my fingers through his.

I'd always felt safe with Jacob. He respected my reluctance to talk about my past and embraced who I am now. It was the first time in my life that I felt I could truly be who I was and not who others expected me to be. I was whole with Jacob.

But do I still trust him?

He's obviously hiding something, something that I know nothing about. Something that led to this. Something bad. I feel like screaming. Running. Escaping. Imploding. My mind races, trying to recall anything else that would've hinted that Jacob isn't the man I think he is.

Tears stream down my face as I straighten. I take a deep breath through my nose and nearly vomit from the smell.

Where is Jacob? Is he dead? Is that why there is a stranger's corpse staring at me in my bedroom closet. I can't stay here any longer. I step as far over my victim as I can. My big toe touches the edge of the blood puddle, squishing into the warm soggy carpet.

Oh. My. God.

3

I hurry to the bedroom door and peer out. Silent. At
least, I think so, but my hearing hasn't completely
returned, so I can't be sure. I step gingerly into the hall
with the gun in front of me. I peer into the spare bedroom
across the hall. The closet doors stand open, its contents
spread all over the floor. The bedding has been ripped
from the bed; the mattress sits askew. I creep as quietly as I
can down the hall, my toes sinking into the white carpet. I
glance into the guest bathroom. The medicine cabinet
hangs open, pill bottles and travel-sized toiletries are all
over the countertop and floor. The master bedroom must
look the same. I'd been in such a hurry to escape the death

room that I hadn't paid attention.

The first thing I see as I round the corner to the living room is Rex lying on the white tile floor in a puddle of his own blood. I watch his chest, willing it to rise and fall, but there's no movement. No! I crouch down beside him and reach my hand out toward him. I can't bring myself to touch him. "Rex, my poor boy."

"Oh, thank God!" Jacob says, leaning heavily on the wall in the living room. Back pressed against the wall, he slides down to a seated position, leaving a red smear in his wake. He uses his hand to soften his landing, leaving a bloody handprint on the white carpet.

At the sight of him, I no longer think about who Jacob really is. No matter what his real name is or what his past might be, he's still my husband.

Three men lie between us. Two had obviously been shot, while the third, who was also clearly dead, had no sign of an injury. At least, he hadn't bled much, if at all. Giving the bodies a wide berth, I make my way to Jacob.

"Oh my God, Jacob," I kneel beside him. Blood seeps through the front of his shirt. "You've been shot," I murmur. Saying those words out loud don't make them any more believable. He reaches his shaky hand toward me and gently brushes my wild hair out of my face. "You did it. I'm so proud of you."

I'm not proud, just sick. How will I live with what I did to the man in my closet? He must've had a family, people that love him, perhaps even children. For a moment, I wish that I'd let him kill me. That would be easier than having to carry his death around with me for the rest of my life. But I'd promised Jacob, and I always keep my promises.

"Oh God...you need...you need to go to the hospital." I jump to my feet to get the cordless phone.

"Katie, wait," Jacob says. "I need you to help me first."

I look toward the kitchen to where the phone lies on the counter and back at Jacob. I have no idea how I can possibly help him. He needs a doctor. I shake my head. Just before I turn to go to the kitchen, Jacob reaches up, grabs my wrist, and pulls me back down next to him. He leans forward and says, "I need to make sure the bullet went all the way through. Is there a hole back there?"

Steeling myself, I look closely at the wound just below his hip. "Yes."

"Good," Jacob says. "You need to help me dress it. Can you get my backpack?"

His backpack? The backpack? The one that I'd never seen before this nightmare of a night? The one that has passports with Jacob's picture and different names? The one sitting in the same closet as the man I killed? Everything in me screams out to avoid having to see the body of my victim. I can't do it. But, I have to.

I hurry down the hall back to the place that my identity took a giant turn from innocent wife to killer. Hopping over the dead man, I grab the backpack. It's heavier than it looks. What's in this thing? As I head back to Jacob, I want to ask him about the backpack, the passports, and hidden guns. I need to know what's going on. But I also don't want to. If I don't know, I don't have to make decisions about what to do next. I don't have to consider the question, if Jacob isn't Jacob then who am I?

Inside one of the compartments of the pack is a small but well equipped first aid kit. Jacob coaches me through dressing his wound. "I think that will hold until the ambulance gets here," I say.

"I can't be here when the police arrive."

"What? Why?"

Jacob bites his lip. "I can't tell you everything right now. I just need to get out of here before—"

Anger bubbles to the surface. "You can't just leave. You need a doctor, Jacob! You need to be in a hospital!" I storm into the kitchen and dial 911. When I return, Jacob is standing at the sliding glass door wearing his jacket, holding the backpack in one hand, and opening the door with his other.

"Jacob, don't."

Jacob stares out the open door. Bitter wind and snow flurries rush into the room, causing goose bumps to appear on my arms. "I didn't want this for you," Jacob says. He shakes his head. "You're gonna hear a lot of things about me—a lot of horrible things. But as you do, please remember—" He turns his head toward me, meeting my eyes. "Katie, you know me." And he leaves.

I rake my fingers through my hair and hold my head. What the hell just happened? *Katie, you know me.* The reverend had spoken those very words to me. I'd mistakenly believed him. I won't make that mistake again. I hadn't known my father back then, and I don't know my husband now.

But I love Jacob with everything in me.

The sound of sirens grows louder as they near my house, breaking my trance. I glance to where Jacob had been sitting. The gun lies on the floor. Never set down a loaded gun.

I pick up the gun and head toward the front door.

I don't stop to grab a jacket or put on shoes. I step out on the front porch and down the steps onto the sidewalk. Two police cars are stopped in front of my house, the blue lights flashing and sirens blaring. I feel as if I'm lying on the bottom of a swimming pool staring at the lights above the water, the sound of the sirens reaching my ears in a muffled way. The events of the last hour flash over and over in my mind faster and faster until they all collide into one gigantic explosion of confusion. *Katherine, wake up…If any of them gets past me, you have to take care of them…*The backpack and the passports…Squeezing the trigger…The man sprawled on the floor of my closet…Rex lying motionless in the red puddle…*I can't be here when the police arrive…Katie, you know me.*

I want to press my hands over my ears to block out the sound, but I know it's not possible. I can't block out what's inside my head. Sirens. Shouting. Lights. My vision dims, and I feel as if I might black out. A familiar voice reaches me over the shouting officers and sirens.

"Katherine," Rebecca says. I turn to look at my neighbor. "They want you to put the gun down, Sweetie."

"Drop the gun!" I notice the for the first time a police officer standing behind the door of his cruiser pointing his weapon at me. "Now! Drop it now!"

I look down at the gun in my right hand. My grip tightens. I shake violently. Open your hand, Katie, I tell myself. As I squat to lay the gun on the ground, I notice the contrast of my blood covered bare feet next to the white of the newly fallen snow. I will my hand to release the Glock and stand, wiping the death off my hands and onto my t-shirt.

"Turn your back toward me and step away from the gun!" the officer commands. "Do it now!"

I comply. Only it's not a conscious compliance. My body responds to the commands without the consent of my brain. I kneel in the snow as the officer clamps handcuffs around my wrists. As I stand, I lock eyes with Rebecca.

"Katherine, are you hurt?"

Am I? "They killed Rex."

The police officer next to Rebecca asks, "Is that her husband?"

"No," Rebecca says. "It's her dog."

The officer leads me toward the cruiser. His voice is soft when he asks, "What's your name, Ma'am?"

"Katherine," I whisper.

The officer leans his head closer to me; I assume to hear me better. "Katherine what?"

As I take in my surroundings, I'm shocked to see so many police cars in front of my house. Five. Five police cars are here in response to my 911 call. What did I say to elicit this much reaction? I can't remember. Everything seems to be moving in slow motion. As I turn my head, my brain doesn't register what my eyes are seeing. It's stuck at what I just turned my gaze from.

"What's your last name, Katherine?"

His use of my name stops me in my tracks. I look at him for the first time. He's not a tall man, though taller than me. His short-cropped hair is either blond or gray; I can't tell with the lights flashing in the dark. A crease runs down the center of his forehead and his brows are pulled together in a show of what seems to be real concern.

"It's so loud," I say.

The officer straightens, waves his hand, and shouts something that I don't register. The sirens stop. "Your last name?"

A hot tear escapes down my face. "Varga," I say. "Katherine Varga."

"Do you live here?"

I look down at my feet and realize how much they hurt resting on the snow. My teeth chatter as I say, "I'm cold."

"Let's move to the car," the officer says. "Is this your house?"

I nod.

"Ma'am?"

"Yes. I live here."

Leaning closer to me, he says, "Are you hurt?" I furrow my brow. What did he just say? "You're covered in blood."

I look down. My once white t-shirt is now crimson. "It's Jacob's blood." So much blood. Too much. God, Jacob, where are you? Why did you run? He won't survive long without medical treatment. He might already be dead.

The officer places his hand on my head as he helps me into the back seat of the cruiser. "Who's Jacob?"

I'm shaking so hard, I'm afraid my bones might break. Whether it's from the cold or the situation, I'm not sure. Looking at the officer, I say, "What's your name?"

"Sorry," he says. "I'm Officer Burns." I nod. "Who's Jacob?"

If only I knew. "My husband."

"Is he in the house? Does he need medical attention?"

Two questions. I'm not sure which one to answer. "He's gone," I say.

"What do you mean gone," the officer asks. "Is he dead?"

My eyes widen. Is he? I shake my head. "He left."

"Why?"

Scrunching my forehead, I say, "What?"

"Why did your husband leave?"

I let out a stomach clenching sob. "I have no idea."

Several long seconds pass before Officer Burns speaks again. "Is there anyone else in the house now?"

I stare at Burns for a few moments. "They broke into our house, and Jacob handed me a gun and told me to hide in the closet. He said that if anyone found me, I needed to shoot him. 'It's him or you,' he said." I shake my head.

"Are the men still in the house?"

"Yes."

"Do any of them need medical attention?"

"No," I say. "It's too late for that."

The officer shuts the door and moves to speak with a group of officers.

The heat of the car thaws my frozen limbs, and at the same time something releases inside me. I lean forward, rest my head on the back of the front seat, and weep.

Everything inside me feels shredded. Everything I thought was true about my life, about Jacob, is a lie. The foundation of my new life proves to be a false bottom. The platform disappears, and I am falling and falling. Where will I land this time?

Several minutes pass. The door of the police car opens, but I can't seem to move. "Ma'am, I'm going to take the cuffs off of you now." The officer's voice is soft, and his hands are gentle as he removes the handcuffs.

"Thank you," I mutter, rubbing my wrists.

"Here," he says, handing me a pair of sweatpants, sweatshirt, thick white socks, and a pair of tennis shoes. "Rebecca brought these for you."

I'm like a starving man who's handed a piece of bread. I pull the socks on first and sigh from the relief. After putting my head through the sweatshirt, Burns says, "We'll need your t shirt." He closes the door and turns his back to the car.

A few minutes later, I'm fully dressed. I knock on the window to let Burns know that I'm finished. He turns, and I hold up the bloody t-shirt. He opens the door and takes the t-shirt with his gloved hand.

"I'm going to take you to the station for questioning, but first, I'm going to read you your rights."

"Are you arresting me?"

He clears his throat. "Not at this time."

As Burns Mirandizes me, I realize two things: in his

eyes, I'm a suspect not a victim, and I've broken the number one rule of suspects. I've answered questions without my lawyer present.

"Do you understand these rights as I've read them to you?"

"Yes."

"Who are those men in your house?"

"I'd like to call my lawyer now."

Burns shakes his head and shuts the car door.

The ride to the police station isn't far. In some ways, it seems to take forever, but in others, it doesn't take long enough. I have no idea what I can tell them. I know nothing about the men who invaded my house. But Jacob does. What had Jacob gotten himself into? I'd been oblivious to anything suspicious. The signs might have been there, but I hadn't been looking for them. I had no reason to pay attention because I'd trusted Jacob. A lot of good that did me. I'm on my way to the police station, my hands still covered in blood, having killed a man.

I killed a man. I shake my head trying to erase the memory of the man in my closet. Unfortunately, the mind is not like an Etch-a-sketch. The picture of my victim's staring eyes and his blood soaking into the carpet has been burned into my brain.

I think about the past several weeks, trying to remember a hint that something like this was coming. I can't. I can't trust my judgment at all. What is it about me that makes me susceptible to dishonest men? This time I won't look the other way. This time I won't avoid the evidence. This time I won't run. This time I'll face whatever truths about my husband head on. Denial is no longer an option.

I can't imagine sitting through a police interrogation. I've witnessed them, taking notes of proceedings for Ed, but have never been the one questioned. I know that the officers will use whatever means necessary to drag out of me any information I know. Only, I don't know anything.

Nothing seems real. Just a few hours ago, Jacob held me in his arms and assured me that everything was fine. I believed him because that's what you do when you trust someone. I wish that I could go back to that moment, to go back to the person I was then. There's no going back to who I was before that man entered my closet just like there was no going back to who I was before my mother's murder. It feels as if I have physiologically changed—as if every cell of my body is different—and I have no idea who I am.

I saw Jacob for the first time a few years ago as I stood in line behind him at the Double Shot Coffee Shop. Actually, I'd noticed him a couple times there before, but we'd never spoken. The Double Shot seemed to always be busy. They served specialty coffee and a different pastry every day. To the right of the cash register sat three black leather couches with oversized comfy chairs facing them, each group forming conversation areas where the shop's patrons could enjoy free WiFi. Several high-top round tables stood on the other side of the shop. A double door was right behind the tables that at this time of the day remained locked. At three o'clock in the afternoon, the doors would be opened to the Double Shot Bar and Grill. I'd only been on the other side of those double doors once while celebrating a co-worker's birthday. It was loud, dark, and crowded. I preferred the light of the coffee shop side.

Just as I stretched to try and glimpse the pastry of the day, my cell phone rang. "Katherine Lewis."

"Where's the Winston file?" Ed Howser never wasted time on pleasantries. He always got straight to the point.

"Good morning to you too, Mr. Howser. The Winston file is on my desk."

"Where on your desk?" The irritation in his voice jumped through the phone. Ed was a walking bundle of anxiety. He popped antacids like they were M&M's. He was also one of the best defense attorneys money could buy.

"Put down whatever you have in your hand and back away from my desk. I'll be there in fifteen minutes."

"But I need it now."

I'd been at the coffee shop for nearly five minutes, and the line had hardly moved. There were only two people in front of me, but by the confused look of the new girl behind the counter, it could be a while. "I thought that you didn't have to be in court until this afternoon."

"I don't," Ed said. "I need to look it over one more time before meeting with Richard at 11:00."

"That's three hours from now." Surely, I could get my coffee first. I needed my coffee. He would just have to wait. Except, I knew that he wouldn't. "Please don't rummage through my desk again. I know exactly where the file is, and I will have it on your desk in precisely…" I animatedly looked around the tall guy in front of me. The line hadn't budged. I suppressed a sigh. "Fifteen minutes."

Ed made a growling sound in his throat, and I knew he was trying not to lose his temper. My desk had an order to it. Every piece of paper, writing utensil, and paper clip had its place. I hated it when anyone touched my things.

The man in front of me stepped to the side and gestured for me to move in front of him. I allowed myself to look Jacob in the face. He was grinning, revealing his deep dimples. I felt my face flush a bit. I smiled back and inched forward. "Ten minutes," I said.

"Fine."

"Don't mess up my desk. You know how that makes me grumpy."

Ed chuckled. "That, I do." He disconnected without saying goodbye. Typical.

I ordered a White Chocolate Mocha, extra-large, and gave the frazzled cashier my name. I pretended to be interested in something on my phone to avoid talking to the tall handsome man who so generously let me cut the line. The sloth preparing my morning nectar irritated me. Didn't she know that most of the customers were already late for work because of her?

"Kate," the girl said dragging the A out unnecessarily.

"It's Katherine," I said too forcefully and regretted my tone immediately. "I'm sorry. I'm just in a hurry."

The girl stared at me for a moment as if it took time for my words to hit her. The girl smiled and said, "Have a nice day."

As I turned to leave, I nearly ran into Jacob. My face grew hot. "Thank you for—well, you know."

Jacob grinned. Those dimples. "No problem."

The next day Jacob met me just inside the door of the Double Shot with two cups of coffee. "White Chocolate Mocha?"

"Um, yeah."

"I'm Jacob Varga," he said, holding out the cup to me.

"Thank you," I said squinting my eyes. "I'm um—"

"Katherine, not Kate. Right?"

I laughed. "That's right." I bit my lip and shifted my weight back and forth between my feet. It had been a long time since I'd talked to a man outside of work. For that matter, it had been a long time since I'd talked to anyone outside of work. My life consisted of a strict routine. My alarm went off precisely at 6:00 a.m., and I allowed myself to hit the snooze button only once. I ate two pieces of peanut butter toast with a glass of two percent milk. I was showered, dressed, and out the door by 7:30, making it to the coffee shop by 7:40. Standing in line was built into my schedule, and now that Jacob had my coffee ready when I arrived, I wouldn't have to rush to make it to my office by 8:00. My nerves jumped. I wanted to turn and run from the awkward situation but somehow managed to stay put.

I should say something, but my head spun, and my stomach clenched. "Um—you really didn't have to buy me coffee."

Dimples. "My pleasure." Jacob gestured toward door. "Let's walk."

"Okay." We stepped outside and I said, "Actually, I work right across the street."

"I know."

"How do you know that?"

Jacob hesitated as if he weighed how he would answer. He smiled. "I work in the same building."

My scalp tingled and my face burned. "How did I not know that?"

Jacob shrugged. "You really should pay more attention to your surroundings."

I found out later that he'd been watching me walk to work for a few months. Jacob had a small business called Secure Data that protected his clients from identity theft on the floor below my office. He'd been working there for a couple years, and somehow, I hadn't noticed. About the third day of Jacob buying my morning coffee, I took a sip. "Ow. That's hot. Is yours this hot?"

"I don't know."

I tilted my head down and looked at him as if I were looking over a pair of glasses.

Jacob laughed. "I hate coffee."

"Then why do you buy it every morning?"

Jacob looked to the side for a moment and then smiled. "It makes my receptionist much easier to work with."

At the time, I wasn't sure that I believed him but soon forgot about it. Jacob bought my coffee every morning after that and walked with me across the street. After a couple weeks, we had lunch together, which led to dinner. It felt like our relationship moved slowly at the time, but, we were married within the year.

It didn't seem too soon. It just felt like the obvious next step. I hadn't been able to feel much of anything since my mother's murder. Jacob pulled me out of that black hole, and not only had I fallen in love with him, I felt hope again, something I thought would never be possible. I trusted Jacob. Now I know that I shouldn't have.

I remember the mysterious smile Jacob had that day more than three years ago. The way he hesitated when I asked him how he knew where I worked stirs something inside me. He'd been hiding something back then, something that I still know nothing about.

Part of me wishes I could run, like I did before, and never look back. I can't do that this time. No matter what the truth is about Jacob, I have to know.

When we get to the police station, I'm taken to a phone. Officer Burns stands next to me. I stare at him. He stares back. "Can you give me some space?" I'm not sure if I'm supposed to be provided privacy for this phone call to my lawyer, but I'd prefer he didn't overhear the exchange.

Burns's eyes narrow a bit, considering. "I'll be right over there," he says pointing across the room, as if he's thinking I'm going to try to escape. I'd love to do just that, but it's not an option.

I turn my back to Burns and dial the number. "Ed

Howser." Ed's voice is scratchy and gruff. I've obviously woken him.

Emotions overwhelm me when I hear the sound of his voice. "It's Katherine," I say, my voice barely registers. I clear my throat. "It's me, Katherine."

"What's wrong?"

I wish there was a way that I could say what I need to without alarming my boss, but there isn't. "I killed a man."

"What?"

I start to cry again, and my words tumble out of me. "Jacob said that if anyone gets past him that I needed to take care of him, and I did. I shot the man in my closet. He's dead. I killed him."

"Holy shit, Katherine. Where are you?"

"The police station."

"Don't say anything. I mean it, Katherine. Don't tell them anything." I hear rustling on the other end of the phone, and I'm pretty sure that Ed's getting dressed. "I'm on my way."

I'd been in this particular interrogation room before. Who was that client? Brian Glover. A nineteen-year-old kid from the Historic East End. How this rich kid got mixed up with gang bangers committing an armed robbery on the south side of Charleston was never clear. He sobbed through his whole interrogation, successfully convincing the arresting officers that he didn't know the guys he was with were going to rob the place. Whether he was guilty or not, I don't know, but he got off without a spot on his record. The other two guys got ten years.

What percentage of those questioned in this room are actually guilty? My guess is that number is pretty high. Even though I work for a defense attorney, I believe that the police usually get it right when they arrest a suspect. As far as Ed is concerned, it doesn't matter who the guilty ones are when it comes to his own clients. They're innocent until proven guilty, and he'll do anything in his power to make sure that his clients are treated that way.

If most of the people questioned in this room are guilty, what does that make me? The minority? An exception to the rule? Although, I did fact kill someone, so I guess I'm not completely innocent. It may have been self-defense, but my victim is still dead.

The walls in the interrogation room are dingy white. I'd assumed, when I was here before, that they were dingy because they were dirty. However, as I study the blank walls, I realize that they are actually pretty clean. But, why white? Why not a calming color like baby blue? Resting my chin in my palms, I massage my eyes with my fingers. I'm just so tired. I don't know how I'm going to get through the next few hours.

Ed comes into view through the glass door of the interrogation room. When he enters, I want to jump up and hug him. Instead, I curl into a ball on my chair, hugging tightly to my knees. He stops and stares for a few seconds before he says, "Are you hurt?"

What a stupid question. Of course, I'm hurt. My life

has been upended. "No."

"Thank God for that," he says, sitting next to me. "Now, tell me everything as quickly as you can." His voice is so low that I'd be the only one able hear him even if we weren't alone in the room.

I begin with Jacob waking me up and end with him leaving. I leave out the hidden backpack. I'm not sure why. Maybe just to protect Jacob. Maybe I'm embarrassed that I didn't know about the hidden compartment in my closet. Now's not the time to analyze my reasons. I'll tell him later.

"Don't answer any question that I tell you not to." The words that follow are familiar to me. Ed tells them to every client that he represents. "Answer honestly but only the question that they ask. Don't elaborate. Don't speculate. Don't respond to their speculations. And, most importantly, don't answer questions that they haven't asked."

For some reason, those words spoken to me instead of in front of me alerts a primal need to defend myself. "I don't think those words apply here. Those men broke into my house, and I had to shoot the man in my closet." I purposely say shoot and not kill. It's easier to accept. "That's it. That's all I know, so I don't have anything to hide."

"Yes," Ed says firmly. "You do. I've been doing this a lot of years, so you have to trust me about this. Answer only the questions they ask. That's it. Nothing else."

I nod in agreement. The thought of keeping anything from the police makes me uncomfortable, but I know that Ed knows best in this situation.

"Now," Ed says. "Put your feet on the floor and sit up straight. You have to appear confident and sure about your answers. You can't look like an easy target." I comply. "You ready?"

I'm not ready, but I nod anyway. No matter how long we wait, I won't be ready.

Ed steps outside the room for a couple minutes and then returns with Officer Burns. The officer is carrying a note pad and a couple bottles of water. He sets one in front of me before settling on the other side. After a short introduction of all present for the recording device, Burns begins. "Tell me about what happened tonight."

"Jacob woke me in the middle of the night, handed me a gun, and told me to hide in the closet."

"Jacob's your husband?"

"Yes."

"Jacob Varga?"

"Yes."

"What did your husband say to you when he woke you up?"

"He said," I say. I'm not sure if I should tell him Jacob's exact words. Protecting Jacob seems more important than defending myself, which irritates me. "He said that they'd found him."

"Who found him?"

"I don't know?"

I barely get the answer out before Burns fires the next question. "You don't know who'd been looking for him?"

"No."

"He never told you?"

I shake my head.

"I need you to answer the question out loud."

"No. He never told me."

"Okay," Burns says. "He tells you that they'd found him, and then what."

"He gave me his gun, told me to lock the bedroom door, and to hide in the closet."

"Why did he think you'd need a gun?"

I open the bottle of water and take a long pull from it. "He said the men were dangerous and if any of them got past him that I should take care of him."

"Take care of him?"

"Shoot him," I say. "To protect myself."

Burns writes something on his pad and rubs his beard. "He knew that more than one man had broken in?"

"I guess," I say and then mentally scold myself for responding to their speculation. I have to be more careful.

"How did he know they were dangerous?"

44

"I don't know."

"Who were these men?"

"I don't know."

"You didn't recognize them?"

"No." I say. "At least not the man in my closet. I didn't look at the others closely."

"Okay," he says and scribbles more on his pad. "What happened while you were in your closet?"

"I don't know."

"You hear anything?"

"A lot of shouting, my dog barking, and a few gun shots."

"What were they shouting about?"

"I don't know," I say. "I only heard voices, not actual words."

We cover me leaving the bedroom, finding the bathroom and spare bedroom in disarray, Rex, the three bodies, and finally Jacob. I tell him that I dressed Jacob's wound and then called 911. I don't say anything about the backpack.

"Then what?" Burns says.

"He left."

"He left?"

I nod and then remember that my answers need to be spoken for the recording. "Yes."

"Did he say anything to you before he left?"

I look at Ed, and he nods for me to answer. "He said," my voice cracks and hot tears run down my face. My next words betray my husband and break something in me. "He said that he couldn't be there when the police arrived."

"Did he say why?"

"No." I say, my voice barely audible.

"Do you know why?"

"No idea."

"Did he say anything else?"

I close my eyes and see Jacob standing in front of the open sliding glass doors. You're going to hear a lot of things about me—a lot of horrible things. But as you do, please remember. Katie, you know me. I shake my head and say, "No. He didn't."

I wake with a start. I open my eyes slowly and see—pink. Pink ruffle and lace curtains. Pink floral wallpaper. I slam my eyes shut. Where am I? Then it all comes crashing back, and I wish with everything that I am that I could fall back to sleep—to oblivion. I look around Ed's guest room and try to take in some of the cheeriness that its decoration displays. I can't. On the chair across the room sits a stack of clean clothes. At first I wonder how Ed was able to get into my house to retrieve them but then realize that the clothes are not mine. I grab the stack and step into the guest bathroom.

I take a long shower, letting the hot water scald my skin in order to awaken a different sensation than the feeling left behind by Jacob. It's like losing my mother all over again; only this time the one I lost didn't die. He abandoned me with a houseful of dead bodies and a street filled with police officers. How dare he leave me to deal with this mess alone.

The water starts to run cold, and I force myself to exit. I dress slowly, carefully, as if I move too quickly, something will explode. The jeans are a little big, but they'll do. The pink blouse is something that I would have never chosen, but I appreciate having something to wear besides Rebecca's sweatpants. I look in the mirror and wonder if I'll look different now to everyone else or just me. I look older, worn. It's more than exhaustion. It's deeper…darker…heavier. I brush through my hair with my fingers and pull it back into a ponytail. I have no makeup, so there's no way to hide my…change. I glance at the alarm clock on my way out of the bedroom and notice that it's almost noon. How did I sleep this long?

Ed and his wife, Sharon, sit at the kitchen table, and I know that they've been talking about me. "Good morning," Sharon says.

"Barely," I say. I mean that it's barely morning, not that it's barely good. There is nothing good about today. Looking at Ed, I say, "What are you doing home?"

"Burns called. He wants you come into the station at 3:30," Ed says. "He said he has a few more questions. We have a little bit of time to go over what happened last night more thoroughly."

"Ed, let the girl eat something," Sharon said. "You must be starving, Katherine." The worry on her face makes me uncomfortable.

I am hungry, but at the same time, I don't feel like eating. "I don't know if I can eat right now."

Ed spoke up. "You may not want to, but you must. You need to keep up your strength in order to get through this." He gives no room for objection. I know he's worried about me too, but he's all business.

I eat a turkey sandwich without tasting it. It does make me feel better. Sharon excuses herself to allow us to talk privately. Ed listens without interrupting as I go through every detail from the night before. He scribbles illegibly, to me at least, on a yellow note pad. When I'm done he fires questions at me. I know this technique. He's trying to look for inconsistencies. I know he believes me. His method of questioning is only to prepare me for the ones who won't find my story convincing.

"So, you didn't suspect anything leading up to this?"

"No." I say it with conviction at first. Then I think about how Jacob seemed more obsessed with our home security. "I should have though." I feel stupid.

"Why?"

I told Ed how Jacob was acting strange for a few days and that he had told me not to worry.

"And you dropped it that easily?"

"I trust—trusted Jacob. I knew he would protect me."

Ed is quiet as he looks over his notes. "He must've known who these men were."

"I don't think he did," I say.

"He said they'd found him," Ed reminded me. "He had to know."

Stupid, stupid, stupid. How could I be so gullible after all that I'd been through before Jacob?

"He didn't mention any names or anything that might indicate who these men were?" Ed asks.

As much as I don't want to relive everything that happened again, I know that I have to. I try to remember everything he said to me. "All he said was that the men were dangerous. That was before he even left the bedroom, so I guess he had to know who broke into our house."

Ed stared at me, rubbing his chin. "How'd they get in?"

"I have no idea."

"You said the guy that entered your bedroom was looking for something. Do you have any idea what that might have been?"

I shake my head. With every question Ed asks, I'm forced to face the fact that I have no idea who I married.

Ed presses me about what happened in my closet, about the man I shot, about everything I saw after I left my room. Instead of gaining clarity, the more I talk, I feel more clueless about all of it. "Are we done?" I ask.

He smiles, but it doesn't meet his eyes. "For now." He narrows his eyes and drops his voice. "You did well last night. Neither one of us knows why they need to speak to you again." Ed takes off his glasses, leans forward, and puts his arms on the table. The seriousness in his expression scares me. "My guess is that they discovered something at the crime scene." He nods to himself. "Just remember to only answer the questions asked. If you don't know the answer, then say that. Even if you have to say you don't know the answer to all of their questions."

"Okay," I say. I have no idea what they could've possibly found at the crime scene that I would know about. Something tells me that everything that happened last night is only the beginning.

What is going on, Jacob?

"That's not Officer Burns," I whisper to Ed as I look through the window in the door. Ed reaches and pats my arm. I'd prepared myself to face Burns again. "Is that unusual? You know, to have someone else question me?"

"Not necessarily," Ed says. "Remember that you're not alone here." He hadn't really answered my question. My hands are tightly clasped and resting in my lap. Maybe if I squeeze tight enough I can stop them from shaking and then the quaking inside me might settle.

The larger man on the outside of the window is

wearing a police uniform. He has dark hair speckled with gray, a square jaw, and dark bushy eyebrows over striking blue eyes. His forehead is tight with seriousness as he gives last minute instructions to the other two. One of them leaves. The one remaining is almost as tall as the first, but much thinner. His dark suit and tie stand out only because it's different from most of the officers I've seen in the building. He's younger than the other one, probably about my age, with dirty blond hair and brown eyes. He looks less intimidating than the larger man not only because of his size but because his eyes are softer and his whole demeanor seems more relaxed.

I watch the officers and study the body language of the one in uniform. I'm pretty sure that he's the one in charge of the interrogation. At first, I don't realize what I'm doing, and then I remember how Jacob taught me to tell if someone is lying to me. Ironic. He must not have taught me well because I never knew when he was lying.

"The first thing you need to understand when assessing a person's honesty is a baseline," Jacob had said. "how they hold themselves when talking, whether they talk with their hands and any facial expressions that they use when you know they're being truthful. Usually, people don't lie about their name or where they live, so that's a good place to start."

The larger man on the other side of the door stands straight and uses his hands a lot when he speaks. He touches his forehead often and runs his hand through his short hair a few times in the few minutes he talks to the other officer. He enters the room first, and the other man follows. Both men sit across from Ed and me.

The first man offers me his hand and says, "Hello, Mrs. Varga. I'm Officer Allen, and this is Agent Stuart."

Agent?

Before I could ask any questions, Officer Allen begins. "Thank you for coming in this afternoon. I know you went through all of this with Burns, but I'd like you to tell me about what happened last night."

I look at Ed and he gives me a small nod. I launch into my story. I told them everything that happened after Jacob woke me up until I found Jacob in the living room. I say nothing about the backpack. I still haven't told Ed.

"So, you have no idea who those men were or why they entered your house?" Allen says.

"No."

Allen leans back in his seat as if he wants to appear relaxed. I note the change in body language. "Notice anything different about your husband lately? He ever mention that he might be in some kind of trouble?"

"No. Nothing." I lean forward in my seat and rest my forearms on the table. I narrow my eyes, challenging him to doubt my lie. I realize that I've just given myself away. It's too late to go back now, so I just stay there. Maybe he'll interpret my change in posture as an eagerness to get this over with.

"So, your husband wakes you up, hands you a gun, tells you to hide in the closet, and leaves to face four men

---

on his own."

"I don't think he knew how many."

"But he said that they were dangerous, so he knew there was more than one."

"I don't know."

"Why didn't either of you call the police?"

It's crazy, but until this moment, I hadn't realized that I should have. My face grows hot. "I don't know—I was kind of out of it from being woken up, and when Jacob told me to stay in the closet, I did."

"You're sure you don't know them."

Up to this point, I'd ignored the agent next to Allen. I glance at him. He appears disinterested in our conversation. Why is he here? "No, but you do, don't you?"

Allen lets a smile slip into his tough demeanor. At least, I think it's a slip. It's probably a questioning technique to make me feel...I don't know how. If his intention is to set me off balance, it works. "We have identified the dead men in your house." He stares at me for much longer than is comfortable.

"So?" I ask.

Allen raises his eyebrows.

"Who were they?"

Allen licks his lips and runs his fingers through his hair. I notice a scar that runs from the corner of his mouth to his ear and wonder how he got it. His silence must unnerve Ed too because he speaks up.

"Is there a point to this?"

Allen sits up straight. "Yes, Mr. Howser, there's a point." He nods to a camera that's on the far side of the room. I knew there had to be one in this room, but I hadn't looked for it. A couple minutes later, the officer that Allen had been speaking to before he came in here walks through the door carrying a file.

Holding the file so only he can see it, Allen opens it and pulls out a stack of photos. "You see, the men in your house are known to be connected with the Vasquez family from Jacksonville. Do you know who that is?"

The name Vasquez sounds familiar, but I shake my head and say, "No."

"Interesting," Allen says. "The Vasquez family has been involved in various illegal activities: loan sharking, money laundering, and dabbling in a little human trafficking, to name a few. The head of the family, Enrique Vasquez, is currently serving a sixty-year sentence for his crimes."

I sit back in my chair and reposition my clasped hands in my lap. I notice my foot tapping and will it to stop. He's leading to some big reveal, I can tell, but I have no idea where this could be heading.

Allen takes a breath and blows it out slowly. He places what's obviously a mug shot on the table in front of me. "This is Chris Gomez—Enrique's second cousin. He was

one of the men found in your living room, along with—"
he sets two more mug shots next to the first. "Steven
Pierce and Paul Estrada."

I don't recognize any of the men in the photos. I wait
for the fourth photo, but Allen seems to be analyzing my
reaction to the other three first. I'm anxious to learn the
identity of the man I killed, but at the same time, I don't
want to know. I bite my lip.

"They look familiar at all?"

"No," My voice is barely above a whisper when I say,
"What was his name—the man in my closet?"

Ed put his hand on my arm.

Allen drops the fourth picture. "Victor Vasquez,
father of four, nephew to Enrique."

Father of four. Because of me, those kids will grow up
without their dad. No. If he hadn't broken into my house, I
wouldn't have had to kill him. It's not my fault. Only, I feel
that it is. I close my eyes and try to gather my strength.

"But perhaps what was most interesting was that when
we looked up your husband's name, we didn't find
anything. Not even a credit report. Isn't that strange for a
man that owns his own business? Don't you think that we
should've found something?"

I don't answer the question.

Allen reaches into the folder and pulls out another
mug shot. He lays the picture on the table next to the
others. "Do you recognize this man?"

I nod.

"Who is he?"

I take a long breath and let it out slowly. I can't let him know how much he has rattled me. "That's my husband Jacob."

The corners of his mouth rise slightly.

"Actually, his name is not Jacob Varga; it's Emilio Vasquez.

I can't catch my breath. I was determined to make it through this interrogation without losing it. I thought that I would tell them what I knew and then leave. I hadn't anticipated discovering truths about my husband that I'm not ready to hear.

My in-laws are in a crime family? My husband is a— I'm not sure what my husband is. I'm not sure who Jacob is. I only know that he's not Jacob at all—not the Jacob I know.

You know me. Jacob's words repeat themselves over and over in my head. Only, it's not true. I don't know my husband at all.

Men are talking around me but all I hear is, *You know me.*

Ed's voice breaks through. "I think she's had enough for today."

Part of me hopes that my interrogators will agree, and I'll be able to leave this place and decide what to do from here. Everything in me screams to run and not look back. But I can't. Not this time.

"No," I say. "I'm fine. I just need a minute."

"We'll take a ten-minute break." Officer Allen gathers the photos in front of him and places them in the folder before leaving.

"We don't have to continue," Ed says. "You've given your statement. All of this other stuff can wait."

"No," I say with more confidence than I feel. "I need to know."

I want to go to the bathroom and splash water on my face, but I'm afraid that my legs won't hold me right now. I close my eyes and concentrate on slowing my breathing.

You know me. You're damned right, I know you. You're a liar.

How could I not have known? How could I live with this man for nearly three years, share a home, a bed with this man and not have been the least bit suspicious? People don't usually lie about their names or where they live, Jacob had said. Perhaps that's why I never knew he was lying because I could never establish a baseline. He lied about everything.

When the officers return, Agent Stuart places a tall glass of water in front of me and takes the seat across from me. Officer Allen sits next to him.

The agent was gentler in his approach, less accusatory. He showed me picture after picture of people that I'd never seen, two of them being Jacob's brothers Enrique Jr., or EJ, and Juan. His third brother, Marco, was killed eight years ago during the arrest of Jacob's father and brothers. EJ and Juan were sentenced to six years but got out after four.

Jacob was also sentenced to six years, but his sentence was suspended because of the help he gave in capturing and convicting the others.

Jacob had acted as the enforcer in the family business. When someone wouldn't pay back the money they owed, Enrique Sr. sent in Emilio. Agent Stuart showed me several pictures of my husband's handiwork, pointing out Jacob's signature—dislocating thumbs." Stuart says. "It's incredibly painful and affective."

The turning point for Jacob as Agent Stuart understood it was when Jacob was sent out to deliver punishment to his cousin Antonio. Antonio and Jacob were more like brothers than cousins. Antonio often helped Jacob with his enforcement duties. But when he was expected to turn his tools of persuasion on Antonio, he'd refused. Two days later, Antonio's body was found. He'd been beaten beyond recognition and had to be identified through his dental records.

"At first, everyone thought Jacob had done it—that his father and brothers had forced him to. But the evidence doesn't lie," Stuart said. He laid a close-up picture of Antonio's hands on the table.

His thumbs were intact.

Jacob had contacted Agent Stuart a couple days later and that began the nine-month process of securing enough evidence against his father to send him to prison.

Jacob had been more than just an enforcer in the family business. He was a computer genius and a master of finances. He had every incriminating detail to take down the Vasquez family crime business at his disposal, and he used it.

The family had owned a bar in downtown Jacksonville that served as the perfect front for hiding their illegal activities. The bar had been shut down after the arrest of the Vasquezes. Jacob's mother owns a restaurant across the street that was originally owned by her mother. As much as law enforcement officers tried to find evidence of criminal activities happening through the restaurant, Abuela's, they never found any. The agent suspected that Jacob had found a way to protect his mother.

"All Emilio had to do to escape punishment himself was to testify against his father and brothers, which he did, and then stay in contact with me for the length of his six-year sentence. But he went out of contact four years ago. We've been searching for him ever since." Agent Stuart looked at the remaining pictures in his hand. "I'd lost hope of ever finding him. But then six months ago, I was informed of a murder investigation in North Carolina that occurred last March."

The agent set three pictures of the gruesome murder scene. "Vince and Donny Harty. The Harty brothers are known associates of the Vasquez family, so it was easy to connect them to Emilio." He slid one more photo right in front of me of one of the victims. "Notice anything?"

I did. I didn't want to, but I couldn't deny what I saw. Both of the victim's thumbs were dislocated.

"Do you remember your husband traveling to Wilmington, North Carolina last March?"

I shake my head but am pretty sure he knows that I'm lying. Jacob had taken me to the Carolina beach for my birthday, but to my recollection, Jacob hadn't left my side.

"Mrs. Varga, can you think of any place your husband would go?"

"I have no idea," I say. "He just left me to deal with this mess by myself."

"Well, if you think of any place," Agent Stuart says as he hands me his business card, "let me know."

I nod.

Allen speaks up. "You know, Mrs. Varga, if you know something you're not telling us, you could be arrested for aiding a fugitive? If you know where he is or he contacts you, you have to tell us."

"I understand."

"Mrs. Varga, please be careful," the agent says. "I wouldn't be surprised if your husband's brothers try to get to Emilio through you."

"I can't help them. I have no idea where he is."

"That may be the case for now," Stuart says, "but I got to know Emilio pretty well during our investigation. I don't think he'd leave you unprotected. He hasn't gone far, I can guarantee that, and if his brothers approach you, he'll come out of hiding."

As we stand to leave, Ed asks, "When can Katherine get back into her house?"

The very thought of returning to that place turns my stomach. How can I face all that happened there alone? And that's what I am now: alone.

"The forensic team will wrap up tonight. We'll let you know."

Ed and I ride to his house in silence most of the way. I wonder if he's as shocked as I am or if he's seen this kind of stuff before. I don't ask.

I'd hoped to get some answers about Jacob. Instead, I have more pieces and no idea how they all fit together—how I fit in this. Instead of gaining clarity, I'm left with more questions. I'm not running this time, and I'm not standing by just waiting for someone to give me the answers. I have to be proactive. I refuse to be the victim again. I refuse to believe in someone who betrayed me.

"Ed, is it alright if I take a few days off? I need time to process all of this."

He pats my knee. "Absolutely, Katherine. Take as much time as you need."

I let Ed believe that I would go to Harrison for a few days and see my brother. Harrison is the last place I want to be right now. I haven't spoken to Luke since the reverend's sentencing, and there's no way that I can face him right now. I need answers, and there's only one place I can get them.

Spending nine hours alone in a car is not a good way to forget your problems. Agent Stuart's voice keeps rattling in my head as he unveils secrets Jacob has kept from me—lies that he's told me. I can still see the carnage he left both in the photos of his victims and what I'd witnessed firsthand less than forty-eight hours ago. How could anyone be capable of such brutality?

How could Jacob be capable?

It all seems so contrary to the Jacob I know. Jacob has always been gentle and patient with me. He's never displayed a hint that a dangerous man existed within him. I must be the most gullible person ever to live. There must've been something in Jacob's demeanor that should've warned me.

But as I think about it, I realize that there had been something. Jacob had been training me. He'd masked it as a hobby of his—skills that intrigued him enough that he learned them himself and then pass on to me. But it was more than just a hobby to him. To him, it was a way of life mandatory to his survival.

He taught me to shoot first. I'd always been terrified of guns. When we were dating, Jacob convinced me to go with him to the gun range. I thought that I was only going to watch. I stood a good fifteen feet away with my ear protection on as I witnessed him expertly hit each of the metal targets. I found myself inching closer as I admired his ability. He made it look so easy. Then he turned to me and said, "Your turn."

I shook my head. "I'm fine right here just watching."

He pointed at me and slowly curled his finger, encouraging me closer.

I shuffled forward shaking my head. "Really, Jacob, guns scare me. I don't want to touch it."

Jacob ejected the clip and locked the slide of the gun open. He set the gun on the counter in front of him and pulled me into a hug. "There's nothing to be afraid of." He held my upper arms gently as he turned me to face the gun. "A gun is a tool. Nothing more. Nothing less. And, just like all tools, it can't operate itself. It needs a person to make it work—to make it dangerous." Jacob paused. His breath tickled my neck as he spoke softly. "See it lying on the counter." He stopped talking and just stared. It felt like ten minutes went by without him speaking. He put his mouth right by my ear and said, "No matter how long we stand here looking at it, it's not going to load and shoot itself. It's just a tool."

Jacob stepped next to me and picked up the gun. "This is unloaded. Okay?"

I nodded. He held out the gun, but my arms stayed stubbornly at my sides. He gently lifted my hand in front of me, so I could take the gun. He started to lay the gun in my hand and said, "Now, just because I told you that it's unloaded, doesn't mean it is. You always have to check for yourself. Okay?" I nodded. "You can never trust anyone or anything unless you witness what they're telling you with your own eyes."

He put the gun in my hand and showed me how to check the gun. He took his time explaining everything I would need in order to use the gun safely. He set the empty gun back on the counter and said, "You need a solid stance, with your feet about this much apart." I imitated his stance. Jacob pushed lightly on my shoulders to make sure that I was steady and handed me the gun. Jacob showed me the proper way to hold it and had me practice pulling the trigger a few times while the gun was empty. He then had me load the clip and insert it into the gun.

I held the gun in my right hand with my left cradling the bottom of the handle. "Now you need to slowly squeeze the trigger. If you jerk it, you'll miss. Slow and steady. Okay?"

I aimed for the metal target and squeezed. The gun jerked as the bullet burst from the barrel. So much power. Too much power. I quickly set the gun on the counter and held my hands up.

"Good," Jacob smiled. His expression turned serious. "But, never lay down a loaded gun anywhere. You are responsible for the weapon, whether it's in your hands or on that counter until you entrust it to someone else's care or stow it safely away. Okay?"

"Okay." I picked the gun back up and tried again. Each time I squeezed the trigger, it jerked a little less. I was a terrible shot at first but became better by the end of our practice. I'm not sure when I stopped being afraid of shooting the gun that day. As we were packing up, I said, "That was fun."

Jacob smiled wide. "It was fun, and you did well."

"No, I didn't," I said chuckling. "I barely hit the target when I managed to hit it at all."

"No one does the first time out. I have a feeling that you're going to get quite good at this."

After that day, Jacob and I went to the gun range once a week. Once I could hit the metal target consistently, Jacob pulled out a paper target. "I can't shoot that," I said.

"It's just paper," he said grinning.

"But it looks like a person."

"So."

"I can't shoot a person."

"You're not shooting a person; it's just a target," Jacob said. "I want you to be able to see where your bullets are hitting on the target, and you can't on those metal targets."

"Okay, but can't the target look like something other than a person?"

Jacob laughed. "I'm sorry, Katie, but this is all I have right now."

It was gradual, but eventually shooting a person shaped target became natural. Jacob drew an upside down triangle on the targets, the two base angles on each shoulder and the bottom just below where the bellybutton would be. My goal was to hit as close to the middle of the triangle as possible, and I was good at it—very good.

I'd thought that Jacob taught me to shoot because he wanted to share something he enjoyed. I had no idea that he was just training me to defend myself—that all the practice with the paper targets was to desensitize me to the possibility of shooting a real person. It had worked. Despite my dread and worry as I sat in my closet, I didn't even hesitate to squeeze the trigger when that man entered, and I'm alive because of it.

And Victor Vasquez is dead.

His face flashes in my mind—Victor staring and bleeding in my closet, his eyes frozen in shock and then his expressionless face shown in his mugshot. I'm not sure which is worse, which version of Victor Vasquez seems more human. Either way, he's dead because he entered my closet, and I took his life. How will I ever get over that?

My self-defense training went beyond learning how to use a gun. "The best self-defense," Jacob said, "is to avoid a confrontation in the first place. This means that you always need to be aware of your surroundings." He took me to places with hundreds of people and showed me how to spot people who might be a threat. He then took me to less-populated areas and did the same thing. "Sometimes, the most danger is present in the safest looking places."

"How do you know these things?" I asked one day.

"I love this kind of stuff. The more I read about it, the more I want to know." Jacob shook his head smiling. "I'll probably never have to use any of this stuff, but I'll be prepared if I do." He kissed me on the forehead. "And so will you."

It was a game to him. He'd sneak up behind me and grab me by the arm. At first, I tried to wrench my arm free, but that only made him increase his grip on me. "I know this sounds counterproductive, but instead of trying to pull free, trap my hand like this," Jacob said. He had me grab his arm, so he could show me. He trapped my hand against his arm and spun under his arm. He then had my arm at an awkward angle behind my back. "Once you're here, I could kick the side of your knee and run."

We switched places and he talked me through the same move. Once I had his arm behind his back, he said, "Now what are you supposed to do."

"You said I should kick the side of your knee, but I don't think I can." I released his arm.

Jacob turned and smiled wide. "You are such a gentle soul. It goes against your nature to hurt anyone. But we're talking about your safety. If I were really some stranger with intent to harm you, you can't hesitate to do what it takes to get away." He put his hands on my shoulder and leaned forward so we were eye to eye. "You're small and would be easily overpowered. As distasteful as it sounds, your best defenses are surprise and pain. If your safety, your life is at stake, you have to use what assets you have to escape."

I nodded even though I was pretty sure I could never break someone's knee no matter what the circumstance. I got better at realizing when he approached and reacting quicker until it was automatic. He taught me how to get free if I were grabbed by behind or from the side. To think about it now, I realize that the self-defense game should have frightened me. I thought that his instruction was just something that we could do together; it was an exciting way to spend date night. I had no idea that he was preparing me. As much as I hope to never have to use my training again, I have a feeling that that won't be the case.

I park in a small parking lot next to the restaurant owned by Jacob's mother. By the looks of the other buildings and the number of scary looking people walking around, I can tell this isn't the safest street in Jacksonville, which makes me reluctant to exit the locked car. My heart races—well, it has been since the incident at my house—since the man died in my closet. Despite my hesitation, the Florida sun shines bright, beckoning me to step out into its warmth. When I left Charleston, it was barely thirty degrees. Here, it's in the mid-fifties.

I watch the front door for a while as diners enter and

exit the restaurant. "You came all this way. You might as
well get this over with," I say out loud, hoping it will give
me courage. It doesn't. I get out of the car anyway and
make my way to the door.

A bell hanging on the door jingled as I enter Abuela's.
The wide-planked wood floors are clean but worn. The
walls are covered with wood siding brightly colored in
peach, yellow, and blue. On the wall to the left hang
dozens of what appear to be family photos.

"I'll be right there," someone says from the kitchen.

A large photo of an elderly woman hangs in the center
of the collage. It's one of those glamour photos where you
have your makeup done, your hair fixed, and you wear
elegant clothes. The woman in the photo smiles wide, her
white teeth showing through bright red lips, and amidst
deep wrinkles, her dimples are predominant. I know those
dimples.

I gaze at the pictures looking for—what? A face that I
might recognize? So, this is Jacob's family. Afraid I might
find Victor Vasquez among the photos, I start to turn from
the photos.

A small Hispanic woman approaches and stands next
to me. "That's my mother. This restaurant was hers. God
rest her soul."

"She's pretty," I say.

The woman smiles, "Ah yes, she was. You should've
seen her when she was younger." Her accent is thick, but
her English is good. "She was, how do you say, a

knockout."

"Are you in these photos?"

"Oh, yes," she says, gesturing to a photo just above Abuela's. "This is my family. I had four boys, all grown now, most with children of their own. " A flash of what appears to be sadness shows on her face. I wonder if it's because she doesn't know where Jacob is.

A woman who had clearly been crying enters the restaurant. "Excuse me," she says and walks over to embrace the other woman. She cries as she murmurs in Spanish to the woman.

I study the picture, and I see him—my husband—my Jacob. Only, he's not Jacob Varga in this picture; he's Emilio Vasquez, a stranger. I continue looking at photos, and my breath catches when one photo catches my eye.

Jacob is in a tuxedo standing next to a woman in a wedding dress. He was married. Of all the things I'd learned about my husband, this bit of information unhinges me. I feel betrayed all over again, and for the first time since this ordeal started, I wish I would've never met Jacob Varga or Emilio Vasquez or whoever the hell he is. I clasp my hands together in front of me to still their trembling. My eyes well up, but I manage to keep tears from falling. What else am I going to learn about him?

I take deep breaths to calm myself. In. Out. In. Out. The crying woman is escorted to the back by a young man, and the first woman, Jacob's mother, returns to me.

"I apologize," she says. "We've had a tragedy in the

family."

I feel as if I'd been kicked in the stomach. How did I not realize before now that the events that happened in my home would affect the people in this family-owned restaurant? "I'm so sorry," I say.

"Only God knows why these things happen," she says.

I know why. Those men broke into my house.

"Is this your son?" I ask, pointing to the wedding picture.

"Ah, yes. That is my Emilio. He's my youngest," she says with a sad smile. "It has been far too long since I've seen him. I don't even know if he—well never mind. Let's get you seated."

I want to tell her that her son is alive and well, that he would come see her if he could, but I can't let her know who I am. The last time I saw Jacob, he was bleeding and escaping through the sliding glass door. I don't know if he's alive or well.

I have to force myself to eat at first; I don't want to be rude. The food is delicious, but with every bite, I wonder about the crying woman. Is it Victor's mother? Did I take that woman's son from her? No matter what terrible thing Victor had done, she was still his mother. There has got to be nothing worse than losing a child, no matter how it happened. The fact that he'd broken into my house, killed my dog, and entered my closet made no difference to her, and at the moment, it makes no difference to me. I shot him. I ended his life. I…killed him.

I turn down the leftover box that the waitress offered me. I wanted no reminder of this meal, this place, or the crying mother in the kitchen. But, just because I didn't want it, didn't mean I'd be able to put this visit out of my mind.

Jacob's mother is nowhere to be seen as I pay the bill at the register. It's probably just as well because I don't think I can look her in the face right now.

The moment I leave the restaurant, I feel it—that tingling sensation that you get when you're being watched. I descreetly look around, trying to discover who might be watching. Just as I reach my car, a man steps out of the alley behind the restaurant. He smiles, and I relax a little but not totally. I scold myself for not having my keys out and ready. Jacob would be furious with me.

I keep the man in sight as I rummage through my purse, desperately trying to lay a hand on my keys. I have pepper spray attached to my keychain, and I could use it right now. I sigh as the man disappears around the building next to the parking lot.

I'm being paranoid. No one is watching. I search more slowly for my keys, and just as I feel them, I am grabbed from behind. I try to scream, but the man's hand is clasped firmly over my mouth.

I weigh my options. Trap his hands and spin. The man must know that trick because he's able to keep me from spinning. I could try and slam my head into the man's face, but he is holding me too tightly to get enough momentum to do damage. I bring my foot up, stomp down on the man's foot and elbow him in the stomach as hard as I can.

An oomph sound comes from the man. He chuckles. "Calm down, Katherine. We just want to talk."

I squirm, but the man just grips me tighter. The first man reappears and approaches us smiling. He has Jacob's dimples, only not as deep. When he gets to us, he pulls out a gun and presses it to my side. "Let's go where we can speak freely," he says.

The one man releases me as the one with the gun puts his arm across my shoulders, the gun in his other hand still pressing into my side. The first man takes my purse, leaving me defenseless. I consider trying to escape but can't figure out how. Jacob's voice in my head warns me. "Never let anyone take you to another location." I squirm, but the man presses the gun tighter.

"I don't want to hurt you, Katherine. Just want to talk to you about my brother."

They think I know where Jacob is. If they find out that I don't, I'll be of no use to them. What would they do with me then? "Where are you taking me?" I ask.

"In there," the man says and gestures to the door behind Abuela's.

11

The muzzle of the gun presses on the small of my back as I climb the wooden stairs. The man behind me presses a code in the digital pad beside the door at the top. A green light flashes, and the door swings open.

The room beyond the rickety stairs is not what I'd expected. I scan it, slowly taking it in. The room is elegant, yet masculine. A large wooden desk sits in the center with two leather chairs facing it. The walls and floors are rich dark wood, and everything shines. A large Spanish-style area rug is in the center of the room only covering the space beneath the desk and leather chairs. Three matching leather chairs rest against the wall adjacent to the door. A small closed laptop is the only item on the immense desk.

"Were you expecting a large plastic drop cloth waiting for you?" the man jokes.

I smile weakly despite my fear.

"Please sit," he says, gesturing to the leather chairs in front of his desk. I hesitate just inside the door, watching as the man with the gun makes his way behind the desk.

The other man pushes me gently. "Sit," he demands, and I know that I have no choice.

Once I'm sitting, the man behind the desk sits in the high-backed leather chair. He sets his gun next to the laptop on the desk.

"So, Katherine," he says. "What brings you here today."

"I felt compelled," I say, my voice sounding shaky.

The man smiles, revealing his Jacob-like dimples. "You felt compelled."

I nod.

"What compelled you, exactly?" he asks.

"Perhaps it was the gun in my back," I say.

He laughs. "Clever," he says, his expression growing serious. "You know what I mean, Katherine. What brings you to Jacksonville, to Abuela's?"

Don't show your fear, Jacob's voice says in my head. *If you give into the fear, you won't be able to escape.* "I was hungry."

The man narrows his eyes. "Did my brother send you?"

"I don't know who your brother is."

The man sits back in his chair grinning. "Forgive my rudeness, Katherine. I've forgotten to introduce myself. I'm Juan Vasquez. I guess I'm your brother-in-law." He gestures toward the man standing against the door, "That's my cousin Jimmy."

I wince every time he uses my name. It's unnerving and disarming, which is probably why he keeps saying it. "My husband never mentioned that he had a brother," I say holding his dark gaze, and then emphasize, "Juan."

Juan rubs his chin with his free hand. The other one rests lightly on the gun. "Well," he says, "I guess that shouldn't surprise me. However, you're here, so you must have learned about his family from somewhere."

I say nothing. My whole insides quake, and I have to force myself to keep sitting. My hands are clasped firmly in front of me to keep them from shaking.

"Why are you here, Katherine?"

Why am I here? I really don't know the answer to that. I just felt like I had to. I have no idea where my husband is or whether I'll ever see him again. I still need to know where he came from. Maybe then I'll be able to make sense of how he ended up with me—of why he ended up with me.

If I let these men know that Jacob disappeared, they'd have no more need for me. If I lie, they will know. I'm pretty sure they know how to read people at least as well as Jacob—perhaps better. I have to play this right, so I can learn more about Jacob's past and get out of this room alive. Juan may have joked about the plastic drop cloth, but I'm not sure that he was totally kidding about the potential of me being killed right here and now.

"I just wanted to see where Jacob came from," I say.

"Jacob." Juan smiles. "You do know that's not his name."

"I do now."

"Emilio can be quite clever in his deception. He certainly fooled me, and I'm not easily fooled," he says warning me to be truthful. "But why you? What does he need you for?"

"You might have a better answer to that question than I do," I say.

Juan leans back in his chair and rubs his face with both hands, leaving the gun on the desk. Could I get to it before he reacts? No. Jimmy would stop me if Juan didn't first.

"What should I do with you, Katherine?" Juan asks.

"I think you should let me go."

Juan smiles. "I'm sure you do." He drops his hands and rests them on the desk in front of him. "So, my brother didn't tell you who he really is."

I shake my head.

"Then, how did you know to come here?"

"The police showed me photos and gave me some background information about Ja—my husband's past," I say. "I think they want to use me to lure him out." Maybe if they think I'm being watched, they'll be afraid of getting themselves caught. Although, he could just kill me and get rid of my body. Juan of all people would know how to leave no evidence.

Juan stares at me. I return his stare, but his intensity is intimidating. *Don't break eye contact, Katherine. Don't show weakness.* "Yes," he says. "Perhaps that is the best way." Juan stands. "Jimmy, escort Katherine to her car."

"I can leave?"

"For now," Juan says. I get up to leave. Just before I get to the door, he says, "Katherine, we'll be in touch."

In other words, the Vasquez family will be watching.

It's time I start using my concealed carry permit. Jacob had insisted I get one, but I never wanted the stress and responsibility that carrying a gun would require. After my encounter with Jacob's family, I don't have a choice anymore. It seems that all control over my life has been ripped from me again. Only this time, I'm the one in danger and the only one that can do anything about it.

I'm exhausted when I pull into Charleston but force myself to stop by the gun store. I buy two guns: A Glock 19 like Jacob's for home security and a Glock 42 in blue teal mint for carrying. I know Jacob wouldn't approve of the girly-colored gun, but he doesn't have a say anymore. Even though the gun would be concealed, it didn't mean the gun couldn't be pretty.

I shoot in the range in the back of the gun shop. I'm a terrible shot with my new compact gun. The small size and light weight make the recoil more difficult to shoot rapidly and maintain accuracy. It also doesn't help that I can't seem to keep my hands from shaking. I'm going to need to spend a lot more time at the range before I feel confident in my ability to stop an assailant.

I manage to sleep a few hours at a hotel before getting up early enough so that I can run to the dry cleaners to pick up something appropriate to wear to work.

"I only have a couple items ready for you, Mrs. Varga. The rest will be ready this afternoon," the lady behind the counter says.

I nod, trying to remember what else I would've brought to the cleaners. I usually only have a couple items here at a time, and those items are ready. "Thank you," I say and decide that my stress level the last few days has me forgetting things.

I walk into work, carrying my coffee and trying to act like nothing had changed since the last time I'd walked through those doors. Jenny, the receptionist gives me a pitiful smile as she hands me a stack of messages written in artful cursive on small pink slips of paper, and I realize that I'm not hiding anything. Everything has changed for me. I've changed, and I need to accept that.

I thumb through my messages, stopping at one from Aftermath, stating that my house will be ready for me to return in a week. I do a quick Google search and find that Aftermath is a company that cleans crime scenes. Ed must've called them for me. I make a note to myself to thank him when I see him.

I can't imagine returning home and facing what had happened a few days ago. Perhaps the most difficult part will be that I'll have to face it alone. I'll have to get used to that again. At least I won't have to worry about it for another week.

I pick up the remaining slips. There are four messages that are paperclipped together. When I see who left them, my breath gets stuck in my throat.

Luke wants me to call him. How did he find me? It's not that I did anything drastic to hide from my brother, except changing my last name. I just didn't tell anyone from Harrison where I was going. I left my hometown and all the people I loved behind me in order to escape the horror of what had happened there. My past was to be left in the past.

And now, my past had found me.

I decide to deal with the other messages first. They'll be easier. They also provide an acceptable excuse to continue ignoring Luke. Part of me wants to hear the voice of someone who loves me, someone who hasn't lied to me. The other part of me knows that speaking to my brother would bring up a plethora of painful memories—memories that I'm not sure I can handle right now on top of everything I'm already dealing with.

I get out a pad of paper, so I can make a list for the day. I begin every workday this way. It gives me a sense of control even if it's only an illusion.

My list-making is interrupted by Jenny bringing me a small package. There's no return address. My heart starts racing. Jenny is almost out my door when I say, "Jenny, who brought this package?"

Her forehead wrinkles in concentration. "I think it was just a courier."

"Did he have a nametag?"

Jenny shrugged. "Not that I noticed. I don't think he had a uniform on either."

I force a smile. "Thanks, Jenny."

I stare at the small box on my desk, trying to decide whether I should open it or notify security that a suspicious package had been delivered for me. I pick up the box and put my ear to it. Feeling foolish, I placed the box back on my desk. My hands are shaking as I grab the scissors out of my desk and cut the tape.

Nothing blows up, so that's positive. Inside the box wrapped in bubble wrap is a small flip phone. Under the phone is a small note written in cramped print: Jacob's handwriting.

Katie,

This is a burner phone that you can use to contact me. My number is the only

one programmed into the phone. Please
do not give it out, don't share with
anyone that I've given it to you. I'm so
sorry for everything. I'll be in touch.

I love you,

JV

I quickly shove the phone into my purse, determined
to never turn it on. I consider telling Ed about it but
dismiss the idea immediately.

I can't concentrate. Maybe I shouldn't have come back
to work today. I tap my pen on the pad of paper, trying to
think of items to add to my list. So far, the list contained
only the words, "Return phone calls." I'd been gone for
three days. My list should fill this page.

I jump when my office phone rings. I answer on the
second ring.

"Katherine?" the caller says, and I recognize his voice
immediately.

"Hi, Luke," I say, my heart pounding. I'm pretty sure
that he's calling because of the home invasion. The news
must be all over West Virginia. I'm not sure how much I
should tell him. "Listen. I'm sorry I haven't returned your
calls, but I've been out of the office for a few days, and I'm
kind of swamped."

"That's what the receptionist said, but I thought I'd
see if you were back."

I grab a tissue to wipe the tears off my face. "I'm

back," I say, praying that my voice doesn't crack.

"I've missed you," he says.

"Me too," I say, knowing that there is no way he can't hear the tears in my voice. "As much as I'd love to catch up with all that's going on in your life, now is not a good time."

"I won't keep you long," Luke says. "I know your busy." Luke is quiet for a few moments. "Dad's dying."

That's unexpected. At first, I want to say, "Good," but I don't. Bitterness forces its way to the top of the things-that-stress-Katherine-out list. I don't know what to say that wouldn't hurt Luke, so I just say, "Okay."

"He's got cancer. The doctors don't expect him to live longer than a couple months."

I take a long breath. "He's been dead to me for a while, Luke. You know that."

"I know you tell yourself that, but I don't think that's the case."

"He killed our mother."

"I know," he says.

"How can you still care what happens to him?"

I can hear Luke breathing. "I've forgiven him."

"How, Luke?" My voice raises. "How can you forgive him for strangling our mother?"

Luke is quiet for a few more moments. "I didn't do it for him," he says. "I just can't carry hate for my father and still be productive."

"I guess I'm not as good a person as you," I say. "Is that all you wanted to tell me?"

"Katherine, I need you to do me a favor."

"What do you want?" I say.

"Go see him."

"No," I snap. "I can't. You should know that."

"I know that there is nothing I can say to you to convince you that you need to see him before—I'm just asking you to do it for me. I need to know that I did everything I could to lift this burden from you before it's too late." Luke's voice is calm and gentle.

"Luke."

"Please," he says, "for me?"

"You have no idea what you're asking of me. I'm not sure I can handle looking that man in the face again."

"I think I do know. I know it'll be hard."

"I can't," I sob.

"Will you at least think about it?"

It's as if Luke reaches through the phone and lays a hand on my shoulder to comfort me. The familiar feeling breaks me. He loves me; that's obvious. He believes that I need to face the reverend for my own good; that's obvious too. He just has no idea what reopening that wound would do to me, especially now. "Yeah," I say. "I'll think about it."

"That's all I ask," Luke says. "I'm sorry for upsetting you."

"It's okay."

"Let's talk soon. I want to hear about everything that has happened since I saw you last."

"Okay."

"I just miss my little sister," he says.

"I miss you too."

"Love you, Katherine."

"I love you too," I say and disconnect the phone.

I'm not sure I want to tell Luke about all that has happened to me since I saw him last. Five years is a long time. Our relationship was strained back then. I haven't seen him since I spoke that day in court. It's been longer than that since we had a peaceful conversation. Maybe it's time to open a door to that relationship again. I'm just not sure that I am strong enough to do what he asks.

Five years earlier

My heels click on the tile floor as I make my way to the courtroom. I'd already legally changed my last name to Lewis, my mother's maiden name, secured a job in Charleston, West Virginia, as a legal secretary, and signed a lease for a cute studio apartment just a few blocks from my new job. I'd broken off my engagement with Jordan; he couldn't be part of my future. Nothing from my past could be. Testifying about the impact my mother's murder has made on my life would be the final step—the final blow that would bring down the house of cards that was my life up to this moment. After this, I could attempt to rebuild. I would leave Harrison, drive the two hours toward my future, and never look back.

"I can do this," I say out loud to myself as I reach the courtroom. My brother Luke sits with Jordan just behind the table where in minutes the reverend will take his seat. I avoid eye contact with them as I sit in the back row on the other side of the courtroom. I'm not on their side today. Luke and Jordan want leniency—a chance for Reverend William Baker to walk free one day. It was God's job to judge the man for his sins. His family should want the best for him. His family should be able to forgive him no matter what he'd done. Besides, they couldn't be absolutely sure the jury had gotten it right. I know they have. William Baker does not deserve leniency. He deserves to suffer.

My ears ring from the pressure built up in my head. On the outside, I look composed, put together, at least I hope so. On the inside, every bone, every organ quakes. Ever since I first laid eyes on my mother's body, I've felt as if my stomach sat sideways. I haven't been able to shake the ever-present nausea, nor have I been able to take a full breath since that spine chilling day. Perhaps I never would.

The judge reads the verdict. Reverend William Baker had been found guilty of the second-degree murder of Anna Lynn Baker, my mother. Judge West asks the defendant if he has anything to say before he is sentenced. The reverend stands and says, "Yes, Your Honor. I did not murder my wife. I loved her, and I could never—" He clears his throat as if he were fighting back tears. I know better. "I'm innocent." He sits down and folds his hands in front of him.

His infuriating words do not surprise me. They were uttered by the man more times than I care to remember. I'd believed them wholeheartedly at first. I'd said the same words to the press on more than one occasion in defense of my father. But there was no denying the evidence. My father murdered my mother.

I pick at a piece of lint on my perfectly pressed black skirt. I notice a chip in my nail polish on the index finger of my right hand—a crack in the shell of my disguise. It is the only outward sign of my brokenness. I barely register the judge calling me forward. My grandmother's rosary is tightly wrapped around the same hand that I hold the paper containing my impact statement.

How does one come up with an impact statement? How can someone put into words the effects of a loss such as this? Mine had been a happy childhood. I lived in a cute little house with a white picket fence across the street from Harrison's Christian Church, where my father was pastor. Evenings were filled with Bible reading and family prayer. I had always believed that my parents had a perfect marriage. They never fought, at least not in front of Luke or me. My parents had the kind of marriage I dreamed of having with Jordan one day. After all, Jordan was studying to be a minister just like my father.

It wasn't until after my mother's death that I noticed a fissure in my parent's relationship. When I really thought about it, I remember walking in during heated conversations on more than one occasion. At the time, I just thought it was normal. Every marriage had disagreements, didn't they? My parents' conversation would end abruptly when I entered the room, which made me uncomfortable but not worried.

I'd always looked up to my father. He was the perfect example of how one should live a Godly life. I remember riding on my father's shoulders as he walked across the street to the church before Sunday services. He would tell me to "find the miracle," and I would have to point out something new every time, like the way the light of the morning sun would glisten on the dew covering the leaves on the trees or the sound of birds singing or the cry of our next-door neighbor's newborn baby. The reverend loved newborn babies. He said that they were so newly formed by the hands of God that they gave off the scent of heaven. "It's the closest that we'll ever be to God's touch in this life," he used to say.

Every Sunday, right after the service, Reverend Baker would step off the altar, gather his little family in his arms, and kiss my mother right in front of everyone. No one who knew the reverend would ever believe that he was capable of murdering his own wife. Except the police. They were the only ones who could see past the façade he presented. They were the ones who'd uncovered the lie that my life had been.

How can I describe losing my mother in this manner? It was just so sudden. One night my mother and I were making wedding plans, and the next afternoon, I found her dead. No matter how hard I've tried to forget it, every time I remember my mother's face, I see the way she looked as she lay on the floor of the church's office, her eyes halfway open, her mouth agape, my grandmother's rosary clutched in her hand. I'd shaken her, trying to rouse her, and screamed.

Losing my mother is like having a limb severed. The pain was instantly excruciating and debilitating. I feel off balance, trying to compensate for the absence of my mother. Nothing would ever seem normal again. Every morning, my first instinct is to call my mother like I used to. My days no longer have order—just seemingly endless hours of bearing the weight of my mother's absence. If only I could hear her voice once more. If I'd known that our morning phone call on the day of the murder would be the last time I would hear my mother's voice, would it have been easier?

Probably not. There's no getting past the grief.

I step up to the podium. "Thank you, Your Honor, for allowing me to speak today." I close my eyes for a moment and swallow hard. I lick my dry lips and clear my throat, just like the reverend had, which irritates me. My face burns as it always does when I am angry. I know that it's glowing red. There's nothing I can do about that.

"As I put together my statement for today, I found it extremely difficult to find words strong enough to encompass the impact my mother's murder has had on me. First, there was the shock that anyone would want to murder such a pure soul. My mother was the most caring person I will ever know. I could stand up here and list all of the positive ways in which my mother affected our family, our church community, and the people of Harrison, but I will spare you the time and only speak of how I personally have been impacted.

"It wouldn't be enough to say that my mother was my best friend. She was the foundation of everything in my life. I looked to her for advice, support, and love in everything I did. I spoke with my mother more than once each day. The utter emptiness I feel every moment of every day now that she's gone is indescribable. I would love to say that I feel her presence or that I know that she watches over me as most people do when they lose someone so important to them, but I can't. I can't even remember the details of her face. I carry her picture with me wherever I go just so I can remind myself how her eyes lit up when she smiled, how one dimple in her cheek was more prominent than the other, or how one clump of her bangs always fell into her eyes.

"At first it was easy to remember how it felt to be held by her. Now, I can only remind myself that in her arms, in her presence, was the safest, best place to be. Sometimes I get caught up in the never agains or the never evers. Never again will I hear her voice on the phone. Never again will I see her throw her head back and let out a laugh that seemed to come from her toes. Never again will I see her cry for me or with me or glimpse the pride she felt for me. My mother will never see me get married. She will never hold my children. And I will never be able to comfort her in her dying days.

"All of these things, the reverend stole from me the day he murdered my mother." I squeeze my eyes shut trying to hold my tears at bay. I know if I start crying, I won't be able to finish what I came to say. I clear my throat. Damn it. "Your Honor, I ask that Reverend William Baker receive the maximum punishment for his crime. No punishment will be enough to make up for what he took from me, my family, and the whole community of Harrison. With your permission, Your Honor, I would like to address my final statements to the reverend." Judge West nods.

I force myself to look at my father. Seeing him sitting there, looking like the victim enrages me. I narrow my eyes and clench my jaw. "They say that anyone is capable of killing someone under the right circumstances. I would've never believed it if it hadn't been for you. I could beg you to tell me why you murdered my mother, your own wife of twenty-seven years, but I know you wouldn't answer me. I'm not sure that you have a reason, I mean, how could you? How could you look into the eyes of the woman you promised to love until death before your God, your family, and your friends and squeeze the life out of her? I can't even begin to imagine what it was like for her to be strangled by the man she trusted. She loved you with everything she was, and you murdered her. How could you?

"How can you, Reverend, continue to plead your innocence when you and I know the truth. You, Reverend, who preached mercy and repentance, you, who stood in front of the congregation and condemned all of those worldly sinners, cannot bring yourself to admit your own sin. You are a coward. I'm ashamed to be your daughter.

As far as I'm concerned, I was orphaned a year and a half ago when you murdered my mother. You have stolen my mother, ruined our family, and stripped me of my faith. I'm not even sure how to go on after this. Your whole life is a lie. You are dead to me. If there is a God, may he have mercy on your soul because I sure won't."

I let my tears flow freely as I say, "Thank you, Your Honor." I turn and walk straight out of the courtroom, ignoring Luke's murmuring "Kate" to me as I pass him. I learn later from listening to the news that evening that Reverend West had received twenty years to life in prison. I will never have to think about him again. That doesn't mean that I won't.

I drive around the block a couple times before I have the
courage to pull into my garage. I sit in the car for a few
minutes, taking slow deep breaths to calm my anxiety. I
know I have to go in now, or I may never find the courage
to do so. I reach into my purse for two things: my
grandmother's rosary and my Glock 42.

I hold the gun pointing down next to my leg and open
the door with the hand that has the rosary wrapped around
it. The smell of disinfectant assaults my nose. I step in and
am greeted by a beeping sound. I turn to see an alarm
number pad with a note stuck to it that says, "Kanawha

State Forest."

Jacob and I had visited the state park only once. We'd ridden our bikes for miles and ate a picnic lunch. I'd started packing up our picnic items when Jacob said, "Katie, wait a minute."

I turned toward him to find him on one knee, holding a ring. I put my hands in front of my mouth in that silly way that you see every woman proposed to on social media. I swore I would never do that. I didn't do that when Jordan proposed to me. I'm not sure why. Maybe, I wasn't as excited about his proposal as I was Jacob's.

"I've rehearsed this so many times, but I never found the right words," Jacob said. He went silent.

"Do you want me to say them?" I asked.

He laughed. "I never thought I would ever ask someone to marry me. I really don't deserve happiness. But then I met you." He gently took my hand. "I love you, Katie. Marry me?"

I didn't hesitate. "Yes," I said, believing for the first time that there really was a possibility of lasting happiness. And now I know that it was a lie.

I type in 0218, and the beeping stopped. I'll never forget that sunny day in mid-February. I thought it was the beginning of forever.

I was wrong.

I turn to find a spotless kitchen. That's certainly not the state I'd left it in. Beyond the kitchen, the white carpet had been replaced with the wide-planked scraped bamboo that I'd been eyeing. The walls were now a soft gray instead of the harsh white they'd been before. There's no trace of the violence that had happened here. I can almost convince myself that it had all been a terrible dream.

I walk slowly down the hall, looking in every room without entering any of them. The wood floors continue down the hall and into the master bedroom. I stand in the doorway and just look.

The bed now rests on the wall opposite the door. A new white comforter and gray throw pillows sit atop the bed. The closet door is closed. I stare at the door knowing that I have to look inside, but my feet don't want to move. Don't be stupid. I tell myself, not knowing whether the stupid thing would be to open the closet door or to run from the room. I decide to open the door.

Wood floor, sparkling white trim, light gray walls, and a line of dry-cleaning bags hanging. The dresser had been replaced to hide the hole in the wall. Just like the rest of the house, there's no evidence of the dead man in my closet. I turn to look at the bedroom and decide.

I grab as many of my dry-cleaned clothes as I can and carry them to the guest room. I can't possibly sleep in the same room where I killed. I return to the master bedroom only to lock the door, hoping to seal the horror behind it.

How had Jacob arranged all of this? The feat would've seemed impossible under regular circumstances. But now he's hiding from—I don't know exactly who—and recovering from a gunshot wound.

"How, Jacob?" I say out loud. I walk slowly around the empty house. I've never felt more alone. Being by myself had never bothered me before, but now, it's unbearable.

I sit on the overstuffed chair in the living room and let myself cry. Speaking to Jacob's mother, being in Juan's office, hearing from my brother, and still needing answers from Jacob have me barely holding on to my sanity. And then there's the reverend.

The reverend is dying.

I'm not sure how I feel about that—how I should feel. Do I feel anything about it? The only feeling I have toward my father is fury. Why should I care if he's dying? I've told myself that he was already dead to me. It shouldn't matter to me that his life is ending. But it does, if for no other reason than to get him to admit to what he'd done. I know he murdered my mother, but he has always denied it. If I refuse to see him, I will never get the chance to hear the truth from him. Am I okay with that?

No. I'm not. I throw my head back and yell, "You bastard! You son of a bitch! You better not lie to me again!"

The house returns to eerie silence. I can't stand this. I don't want to sit in this empty house by myself. Nonetheless, I'm alone.

Again.

As I slide into the driver's seat of my Corolla, I notice movement in the back seat. My breath catches. Not the Vasquez brothers again. I drop my keys on the floorboard. As I bend to retrieve them, I slip my Glock 42 out of my ankle holster. I turn quickly and point my gun toward the back seat.

"I know you're back there. Think carefully before you make your next move, because I have no problem putting a hole in you."

"Katie, it's me." Jacob slowly raises his head to look at me while remaining in a crouched position.

I inhale sharply and stare at my husband. Tears threaten, and I blink hard to hold them back. My stomach flutters. He looks good, as if he hadn't been shot just a couple weeks before. *He lied to you*, I remind myself, so I won't lose myself in the warmth of relief. "It's Katherine. What the hell do you want?"

Jacob is sprawled across the backseat, keeping his head low. "I promise I'll tell you everything. First, can you just drive someplace where we won't be so easily seen?"

I sigh heavily and cram the gun back in its holster. More secrets. Secrets and lies are interchangeable to me. The more I learn about Jacob, the more I wonder how much more he's hiding. My stomach is trying to shove itself into my throat. The worst part is that I don't know whether I want this conversation to be over or if I want to draw it out to be with Jacob as long as possible. How can I want to be around a liar?

"I met your brother Juan and your cousin Jimmy." I say, looking through the rearview mirror at Jacob. "Charming, those two."

Jacob's eyes widen, and his face can't hide his panic. "My brothers are here?"

"Relax. Not here. I took a short trip to Jacksonville." I remember the feeling of Juan's pistol pressed into my side. I bite my lip—a nervous habit that I've picked up since last seeing Jacob.

Jacob's mouth drops open for a moment. "Why in the hell did you go there?" Jacob's voice shakes with outrage.

"You have no right to be upset," I say more calmly than I feel. If he'd been honest with me, I wouldn't have had to go there. I hadn't had a choice.

"Turn left up here," Jacob says.

"Your mother's a sweet woman. She misses you though. I could tell." I pause, but Jacob remains silent. "She makes great guacamole." No reaction. "Oh, and my favorite part, I saw your wedding picture hanging on the wall of the restaurant. I'm not sure why I was surprised that you were already married. I should've known."

Jacob's pained expression grows more apparent. He runs his fingers through his hair and sits up in the back seat. He winces. Alternating between staring out the window and glancing at me, he says nothing. His beard looks scraggly and uneven. My husband had always taken great care in his appearance. He looks nothing like the Jacob I know, yet when I look at him, I'm overwhelmed with worry.

"Why me, Jacob? Why did you target me?"

Jacob narrows his eyes. "Target you? I didn't target you. I love you. You're not my victim. At least, I never intended you to be." He looks down at his hands.

"Yeah well, it happened anyway, didn't it?"

"I never wanted to put you in danger, Katie, you must know that."

"Katherine," I growl. "How could I have been so stupid. With my history, you'd think I'd know better than to trust anyone. I'll not make that mistake again. I'd rather die than have another person I thought loved me betray me."

"I didn't betray you, Katherine," he yells. "I could never—"

"You lied to me, Jac—Emilio. About everything! I can't believe that I let myself believe that you loved me."

"I never lied about loving you."

"Whatever, Ja—" I shake my head.

At first, I don't say anything. I can feel my heartbeat in my temples, and I'm sure that my face is crimson. I've never been this furious with anyone before aside from the reverend at least, but never Jacob. "I can't believe how clueless…Well, not anymore. I'll never trust you again."

Jacob is silent for a while, staring out the window. I watch him through the rearview mirror. He rubs his eyes and slowly strokes the whiskers on his cheeks. I've never seen Jacob with a beard. I don't like it. His eyes are watery and distant, and my heart breaks for his misery, which frustrates the hell out of me.

My breathing slows, and my anger loses steam as I watch my husband battle something inside him. "You intrigued me," he says quietly. "I mean, you were always alone, yet it was as if it was your choice to be, as if you didn't mind it. I couldn't tell if you were a wounded soul or just a loner. I was alone a lot too, but not because I wanted it. Circumstances dictated it. I saw something in you that I didn't have. I don't know. I guess when I found out that you'd testified against your father, same as me, that we at least had that in common. If you could move on after that, maybe I could. Maybe I could be content. Maybe I could be a better man than I'd been."

"How did you know that I testified against my fa—the reverend?"

Jacob sighs. "Remember that day in the Double Shot? When I let you in front of me in line?"

I nod.

"I knew your name was Katherine, not Kate." He grins slightly, and I have to look away. "When you answered the phone, I found out your whole name. And, well you know what I do for a living. I researched you."

Incensed, I say, "You did a background check on me?"

Jacob's eyes widen as if my anger shocks him. Shrugging his shoulders, "I just wanted to get to know you."

"Is that how you get to know all of your friends? You dig into their secrets to find out their vulnerabilities? Most people just talk to the person they want to learn about."

Pinching the bridge of his nose and squeezing his eyes shut, Jacob says, "You're right. I'm sorry."

His apology discomfits me. It seems sincere. Vulnerable. I can't let him get to me. He didn't even deny having another wife before me. Where is she now? "Who's Jacob Varga?"

Again, Jacob is taken off guard. "What?"

"You obviously stole his identity. I want to know who he is."

Jacob runs his fingers through his curly hair and clasps his hands together behind his head. "He's a man who died in a car accident six years ago in Nevada."

"You stole a dead man's identity?!"

He narrows his eyes and drops his hands, confused by my question. "He didn't need it anymore."

I glare at Jacob through the rearview mirror. "It's not funny, Jacob!" I can't bear to look at him anymore. "I mean Emilio. Jesus, I don't even know what to call you." Right after those words leave my lips, something slimy creeps up my spine. I would've been grounded for a month if I'd used Jesus's name in this manner if my father had heard. However, the reverend no longer holds my moral compass. To hell with him and how he would feel if he'd heard me. But what would my mother have said? I wish I could wash my own mouth out.

"Call me Jacob. That's who I am now." His voice is soft. "Turn right up here into that parking garage."

My voice is not soft. "That name isn't yours. It belongs to a man you don't even know—a man who is loved and remembered by people who miss him." I imagine if I were to learn that someone else went by the name Anna Baker, and it makes me sick. My mother's name is sacred now that she is gone. To take her name would be to make a victim of her again. "How could you take a dead man's name? How is it even possible?"

Jacob's mouth drops open for a moment, and his eyes tear up again. "Um, I never thought of it that way." He turns back to stare out the window.

I say nothing to this, which makes the silence in the car seem like an increasing cavern between us. I can almost see the crack in the invisible wall Jacob has had around him since I first met him—as if I'm glimpsing who my husband actually is. I'm not just horrified that the man I married had stolen someone else's name; I'm shocked that he could do it so easily. What kind of life had he lived before me that would allow him to manage such a thing? In the rearview mirror, I see the pain that he is attempting to manage, something in me stirs. I want to tell him that I forgive him for everything to ease his torment, but I can't because I haven't. Forgiveness is never that easy, and he hasn't begun to reveal all he needs to for me to consider it.

"Seriously, you have a birth certificate and a social security card. How is that even possible?"

Turning back toward me, "Do you really want to know?"

"Yes."

Jacob straightens himself up more in the seat, wincing as he does. "I got his name from an obituary. Obituaries usually state the decedent's mother's maiden name. I used that information to order a birth certificate."

"And the social security number?"

"They become public once someone dies."

As I consider this, another realization comes to me.

113

"Jose Gomez?"

Jacob sighs. "Died eighteen months ago in North Dakota."

Unbelievable. "Why did you need Jose's identity?"

I pull into a space on the fourth level in the darkest corner of the garage. There's no one in sight. I turn sideways in my seat to face Jacob. Our eyes lock for several seconds before he answers.

"Owning a business under an assumed name is tricky. Most people don't know this, but the IRS usually doesn't pay much attention to businesses that are under three years old." He uses both hands to rake his hair. "Jacob Varga had been listed as Secure Data's owner for right at three years, so I had to sell it. To myself as Jose Gomez."

This just keeps getting better. Who the hell did I marry? "They showed me pictures. Of those men ...the things you've done." I recall photo after photo of the men he had beaten. All of this cannot possibly be true. But it is. "I didn't believe them at first. I couldn't imagine you being able to...do so much harm to another human being."

I couldn't have imagined myself being able to shoot someone either, but I had. "What did they do to deserve what you did to them?"

"It's safer if you don't know."

"Safer for whom, Jacob? I'm your wife!" I shriek. I remember the photo on the wall of his mother's restaurant and let out a sigh. "At least, I thought I was, until I saw you smiling in a tuxedo next to that woman. What about her?

Does she know about me? Or have you been lying to her too?"

Jacob squeezes his eyes shut and shakes his head. Looking at the ring on his hand, he says, "I haven't seen her in over seven years. That marriage lasted all of three months. Neither of us wanted it, but our families insisted. I moved out of our apartment when I started talking to the FBI. She wanted the divorce as much as I did. Maybe even more." He raises his gaze to mine. "I swear to you, I never loved her the way I do you. I never loved anyone before you. I was a different man then. I wanted to forget the marriage had ever happened. That any of it had happened. I am not Emilio Vasquez anymore. I can never be him again."

I believe him. I can't help it. But there is so much I still don't know. "What do your brothers want from you?"

Jacob leans his head against the back seat and stares at the ceiling. "Probably the money."

I hadn't expected that. "Money?"

"When I decided to work with the FBI, I didn't want to be left helpless. Over the nine months I was their informant, I moved money to an offshore account. Because of my skill with computers, I was in charge of cleaning the money that came in through my family's business."

"What business? The restaurant?"

Shaking his head, "No, not the restaurant. The bar. My father owned a bar across the street from Abuela's.

Only, it wasn't his only source of income. Since the bar took in a lot of cash, it was easy to hide what he'd earned from his other…endeavors.

"Anyway, I was able to sneak money into an account. I didn't think they would ever find it, but I guess, after they discovered that I was the mole, they looked closer."

"Where's the money?"

His eyes look worried. "I'd rather not say."

I want to scream. "How much money?"

"A lot."

"How much?" I ask holding his gaze. "One million? Two million?"

He raises his eyebrows.

"More?"

He nods. "Enough. There's enough money there."

"What does that mean, Jacob? Enough for what?"

"To start over."

My head spins. I want to know everything, but I can't take anymore at the moment. "What do you want from me?"

"I want to know that you are okay." Jacob's eyes grow more serious. "You look so thin. Are you eating?"

I glare at him.

"I need you to be safe and you're not safe alone." He shakes his head. "Maybe you should get another dog."

Rolling my eyes, "I carry a gun now. I can take care of myself. And I don't need a dog to protect me either. The security system that you had installed without consulting me will certainly give me enough warning to arm myself."

Grinning, "That gun's a toy." I say nothing. "I just don't like you being alone, Kat—Katherine. The dog is for companionship."

Suddenly, I'm exhausted. I need time to process what little information I've gained. To unwind all of the warring emotions twisting themselves inside my gut. "Where can I take you?"

"I'll find my own way."

"Seriously?" Is it even safe for him to roam around unprotected? I shouldn't care. I don't care.

"I'll be fine from here." Just before closing the back door, Jacob says, "Katherine, I love you."

"I really wish I could believe you."

I back out of the space and look at Jacob through my rearview mirror. I ache for him—not for the man standing in the now empty parking space, watching me leave, but the man I thought I knew—the man I love. How could I be so naïve? Again. I shake my head, trying to break whatever it was that tied me to him. It stretches but doesn't break.

Like whatever ties me to the reverend. I want desperately not to care for my mother's murderer. I've put distance not only from him but also from everything that might remind me of him— or remind me of my mother.

But familial ties are not easily broken, only stretched. As hard as I've tried not to, I think about the reverend and who he used to be to me every single day. I've even tried to ignore the longing I have for my mother, so I won't think about him. I don't want to forget my mother—only the reverend. But her memory is connected to him, not just the fact that he killed her, but because, like it or not, they're both my parents.

Since Luke's call, it's as if I have two movies of my past playing at the same time over and over in my mind. One is about growing up in Harrison, beginning with a happy childhood and ending with finding my mother's body. The other is about my life with Jacob, also beginning happily and ending with the dead man in my closet. In both, I'm clueless to what's really going on—to who the reverend and Jacob really are. The movies play in a loop, and I haven't a clue how to make them stop.

I need answers. And closure, so I can move past—I don't even know what to call it. Death? Denial? Ignorance? As much as I don't want to, I know what I have to do. *Damn it, Luke; why did you have to call now?*

16

I sit waiting for the reverend to arrive. My hands are clasped in front of me on the table with my grandmother's rosary wrapped tightly around my right hand. I'm grateful that they allowed me to keep it with me. I assured the prison officer that I needed it for emotional support. I'm not totally sure if that's true or if I only want it to irritate the reverend. I have no idea what I'll say to this man whom I vowed never to see again. I don't want to be here, but Luke had made it sound vital. I hadn't slept well last night. I kept dreaming about finding my mother all over again. Only now, I know that the reverend's wailing was just for show, which makes reliving the whole experience unbearable. I hate the man that I am about to see. I just want to get this over with.

He arrives in chains. He is a shell of the man that I knew to be my father. His prison garb hangs off his skeletal figure as if he were a boy wearing his dad's pajamas. The dark circles under his eyes only highlight the sadness in them. I have never seen him this vulnerable. The guard gestures toward the chains and nods at me, making sure I am okay with him removing them. I nod back. The reverend's chains are removed, and he sits across from me. He's no danger to me. Of course, my mother probably thought that too.

Let him try.

I wait. I have nothing to say. I'm only here for one thing, to hear the truth from the man who murdered my mother.

"Thank you for coming," he says. His voice is shaky, and I'm not sure if it's from frailty or emotion. I nod and shrug my shoulders. He stares at me as if he's trying to memorize my features. It's unsettling. I want desperately to look away from his stare, but I don't. He looks at my hands and notices the rosary. "Those Catholics, always dwelling on the suffering Christ." He reaches toward the crucifix sticking out of my closed hands, and I jerk them back. He winces, and I know that I've just hurt him. Good.

The reverend sits back in his chair and lets out a sigh. "I never understood why they focused so much on the passion instead of the resurrection. I mean, why obsess over the torture, the defeat, and the crucifixion when Jesus conquered death and rose? I always felt it was more important to focus on the happy ending." He swallows hard and looks down at the table. "Until I ended up in here. It's hard to grasp the joy of it here."

I sit stone-faced. My stomach is rolling, and I feel my face growing hot. I don't want him to see my emotion, but my darn red face always gives me away.

The reverend clears his throat. "I don't sleep well in here. I dream a lot; well," he shrugs, "I have nightmares, mostly about Jesus's torture. One night I'm witnessing Jesus being scourged. With each lash, the metal bits on the end of the whip rip the skin on his back, spraying blood and skin in a huge arch. I watch, entranced at the horror of it, knowing I should look away, but I can't seem to do it. Just when I think I can leave—" the reverend says, looking past me and shaking his head. "I realize that I'm on the other end of the scourge, that I'm the one swinging the whip, tearing his flesh, and something inside me shifts— like a darkness revealing itself. With each swing of the weapon, I long to hear him cry out—to hear him say that it should be me on the receiving end of his lashing scourge. But he doesn't. He cries in pain, but he never pleads with me to stop. He just takes it."

The reverend rubs his forehead. "And I realized that he allowed himself to be tortured and murdered not only for the righteous but also for the one holding the end of the scourge. He died for the ones who pressed the crown of thorns on his head—for the ones who drove the nails in his hands and feet. Redemption is for everyone, even those most undeserving. Like me." He shrugs his shoulders and says, "I guess the Catholics are right on this one thing. Until I contemplated on the suffering Christ, I couldn't appreciate the fullness of his victory."

My father. Always the preacher. But his words shock me. He's always known the answers when it comes to faith. For him to admit that he'd been wrong, well that's just unbelievable. I can't tell if he's sincere or trying to manipulate me into softening toward him. *I'm sorry to break it to you, old man, but it's not going to work.*

"I found God in here. Isn't that funny?" He smiles slightly even though it obviously pains him. "I've spent my whole life preaching about who God is, but I didn't really know him. Oh, I knew the scriptures, but I took to heart only the parts that fit into my image of God—the parts that fit with my image of me." He shakes his head and looks past me again. "Nope. I didn't know him at all until I dwelled on his suffering."

The reverend strokes his face as if he is smoothing the beard he doesn't have. His brows are knit as he sits in deep thought. My father, just like everyone else stuck in this place, found God. How cliché. How predictable. How infuriating.

"Why'd you do it?" I say, breaking the silence.

He's taken aback by my sudden subject change. He doesn't need me to clarify that by it, I mean murder my mother.

He closes his eyes and takes a deep breath. "I don't know," he says. It's the closest he has ever gotten to admitting to me that he was guilty.

"You don't know?" My voice is soft but firm even though I want to scream at him.

"It seemed like my only choice at the time."

I can't take it. "What do you mean, your only choice? I can't imagine any possible justification for murdering my mother. Your wife." I feel the tears try to come, but I can't let them. "What could she have done to you to deserve having the life squeezed out of her by her own husband?" Hot tears stream down my face. I don't want him to see me weak, but I can't stop them from coming. "You're supposed to be a man of God!" That last part is meant to hurt him, and it does. Had he ever truly been a man of God?

The reverend covers his face with his hands and weeps, which makes me want to relish in my success, but at the same time, it shames me. I desperately want to leave, but I haven't fully gotten what I came for. I wait.

The guard comes through the door with a box of tissues. He places them on the table between the reverend and me and pats the reverend's shoulder. The guard's compassionate action toward my mother's murderer discomfits me. For the first time today, I see this man in front of me as someone worthy of compassion, and I hate it. The reverend thanks him and noisily blows his nose.

"This is so hard; you have no idea how difficult this is—to have to face my own daughter and admit what I've done." He wipes his face dry, but it doesn't stay that way. "I agree with you; there's no adequate reason for what I did. I can only try to explain my thinking at the time. To this day, I'm baffled by my actions." He swallows hard and continues. "As you know, I was having an affair with someone I was counseling."

"Bonita Scott," I say.

He nods slightly. "Unfortunately, she wasn't my first affair. I didn't realize it at the time, but I needed to be admired. I hate to admit it, but I think this need is what inspired me most to become a preacher. Disgusting, I know." Shaking his head, "Don't get me wrong, I believed everything I preached. It wasn't like I was pretending to have faith in God." The reverend stares straight into my eyes as if he is willing me to believe him. I don't.

"This need is probably what drove me to those other women. Your mother admired me at first. But after being together for a while, that admiration wore off. I didn't realize that genuine love is much more important than mere admiration. I know that now, much too late.

"Your mother walked into my office that day as I hugged Bonita goodbye. She could tell that it wasn't an innocent embrace between a pastor and church member. It was—more intimate.

"She just stood there, just inside my door, waiting for Bonita to leave. Unbelievably, she was gracious toward Bonita and politely said goodbye to her. For a moment, I thought she hadn't realized what had happened between Bonita and me, but as you know, your mother was too smart not to notice." He pulls another tissue from the box and wipes his face. He stares at the wet tissue in his hand and clears his throat.

"She told me that she was fed up—that she wasn't going to look the other way this time. She said that as soon as you and Jordan were married, she was going to leave and that everyone would know of my infidelity. Everyone would know that I was a fraud of a minister—that you and your brother would finally know the truth about me." The reverend grabs his head firmly as if he is trying to keep it from exploding. "Then she said that not only did she regret marrying me but that she regretted believing the lies I had told her about her Catholic faith. She said that she'd been seeing the priest over at St. Paul's for counseling and that she'd been attending daily Mass instead of meeting friends for coffee like she'd told me.

"I don't know, but when she told me that I would be found out, that the congregation and the community would learn about my infidelity—that you and your brother would learn it too, I thought that she would turn you against me."

The reverend squeezes his eyes shut and shakes his head. "I don't know—I just snapped. I yelled at her to shut up, but she kept talking about my secret getting out and about losing your admiration. I grabbed her throat and couldn't let go. I just wanted to shut her up, to stop her from doing what she promised to do. I just…held tighter until she was gone."

Tears fall freely down the reverend's face. "I can't get the image out of my head. The desperate, shocked look in her eyes. It'll haunt me forever. I'll never forgive myself, and I don't expect you to be able to either. I just pray that God has, so I won't get the eternity that I deserve. I'm truly sorry for what I did. I would give anything to undo it. I'm so sorry for all of the pain I've caused you and your brother—everyone."

I'd thought that hearing what happened from the man

himself would provide some relief—some closure. I feel no relief—only rage. "That's it? That's your excuse? You murdered Mom because she was going to expose you? Do you have any idea the enormity of what you've done? You want me to believe that you regret it?" My voice raises with every word.

"That morning, you sat in the middle of the church—just minutes after you killed her. I asked you if Mom was still there. Do you remember that?"

He nods once.

"You said that she was in the office. You knew that I'd find her there. You let me go into the room where my mother lay dead because you thought it would make you look innocent. I mean, what kind of father would knowingly let his daughter discover her murdered mother? What kind of person does that?"

I stand and glare down at him as he curls in on himself. "I trusted you, damn it! I loved you and trusted you. I thought that when you love someone, and they love you that you can trust them. Now I know better. I can't trust anyone, especially those who supposedly love me."

"I'm so sorry, Kate. I'd give anything to be able to undo what I've done."

I chuckle. "You're sorry." I step back from the table. "Do you remember when you told me, 'Be careful with your words, Kate, because the words I'm sorry can't erase the pain your words can cause?'"

He stares at his hands and twists the tissue around and around.

"Do you remember that?" I ask again.

He nods.

"I'm sorry doesn't even begin to make up for this."

He buries his face in his hands again. I should stop. I know I should stop, but I don't. "You took my mother from me. You didn't just kill her. You looked into her face and watched her die. I'm sorry doesn't begin to cover it.

"You lied to everyone, Dad. You lied to me! You let me stand in front of reporters and make a fool of myself defending you. You let me lie for you!"

I plop back down in my chair. "I was so sure you couldn't hurt Mom. There was just no way you could have done it. I walked into that courtroom sure of your innocence, hoping that the truth would be revealed, and you could go home and continue to—" I shake my head. "Well, the truth came out. I was so stupid. The police tried to tell me. But I just thought they were being single minded. It's always the husband, right?

"The evidence against you was compelling, but I still wasn't convinced. Until Bonita Scott got on the stand and said she'd left you and Mom in the office that morning just fifteen minutes before I came to the church. There was no way anyone else could have killed her. It had to be you."

Fury roiled inside me—a growing flaming monster who'd been festering in my gut since that day in the courtroom. I'd never even come close to letting it loose before. But now, with finding out Jacob isn't who I thought he was, just like my fa—the reverend, I can't keep the monster contained. I swing the gate wide open. I lift myself out of my chair and lean forward with my palms pressed firmly on the table between me and the man who murdered my mother. "The truth came out and broke me. Everything I knew about you, everything I trusted about my life was all wrong. You are nothing but a liar, Reverend. You lied to Mom. You lied to Luke and me. You lied under oath and lied at your sentencing. And now that you finally admit the truth, you sit there trying to make me feel sorry for you because you know you don't deserve forgiveness but still have the audacity to expect it. Well, you're not getting it from me." I turn to leave but then turn back to deliver my final blow. "I hope you burn in hell."

I leave him sobbing. He'd looked frail when first saw him walk through the door. Now he looks shattered. Luke is going to hate me when he hears about what I did to this man, the reverend, our father. I tell myself that I don't care. Who's the liar now?

I'd expected an angry phone call from Luke, but I don't get one. I can only assume that the reverend didn't tell him about my outburst. A week after visiting the prison, I get a letter from the reverend. It's short and to the point.

Kate,

I don't expect you to understand or forgive me for what I've done. I know I couldn't if I were in your position. Regret is not a strong enough word for what I'm feeling. I hate myself. I don't deserve forgiveness, and I don't expect it. All those things you said to me, well, they were all true. I hadn't fully faced the whole of the consequences of my actions until you laid it all out there. I know you, Kate. You've always had a sweet nature and a pure heart, and I know that one day you may regret your words. Please don't. I needed to hear them, and I am grateful. I don't have much time left on this earth, and it's important that I acknowledge all that I'm guilty of before I meet my maker face to face.

Please don't be afraid to love or trust because of me. Not everyone is as untrustworthy as I have been. But no matter what evil I have perpetrated, I have always loved you and your brother more than you can possibly know. And, in case you need to hear it, I forgive you.

Dad

As hard as I try, I can't summon the rage monster when thinking about the reverend. When I think about the visit, all I feel is immense shame. I don't want to have to face him again, but I know that I have to if I ever hope to feel any peace. I'm not ready to see him though. I may never be.

I can't think about the reverend right now. I'm barely

holding myself together as it is. I'm just so damn lonely. It wasn't supposed to be this way. Jacob was supposed to be with me through the hard times. Isn't that what we'd said to each other at the courthouse? I could've never imagined what our lives would become. It seemed to happen overnight—just like losing my mother. Only I'm more alone now than I'd been then. I had Luke and Jordan, but I pushed them both away and ran. And now, here I am, with an emptiness so deep and heavy, it sets like a metal ball in my stomach pressing against my lungs, so that it's hard to take a full breath.

I miss my husband. Yes, I know how pathetic it is to miss someone who left me alone to deal with his mess. He says he left to protect me. Is that true, or did he leave to protect himself? I don't know, but right now I'd give anything to have him next to me.

I pull up in front of the Kanawha Animal Shelter. I hadn't planned on ending up here, but I just can't face going home to the empty house again and replaying my visit with the reverend over and over in my head. So, instead of confronting my regret about my father, I'm getting a dog.

I stand in front of the German shepherd puppy. This one would be perfect. He reminds me so much of Rex, and Rex was a perfect protection dog. In the kennel next to this one sits a medium sized golden retriever mix. She stays about two feet back from the gate, her head low and her tail tucked as far under her as far as she can manage. Too timid. I ask to have the German shepherd brought to the meeting room.

The dog is exactly what I came in looking for, but for some reason, he doesn't feel right. Maybe I'm feeling disloyal to Rex by replacing him with another just like him. "He's four months old and already neutered," the shelter employee says as she looks through the puppy's paperwork. The lady asks questions about whether I have any other pets, if I have a fenced in yard, and how I plan on making sure the puppy will get the exercise he needs. She rattles on about the adoption process, but I only half listen.

As I play with the puppy, all I can think about is the shy dog still huddled in the kennel. There's something about her. "Can I see the golden retriever that was next to this one?"

"Are you sure? She's not nearly as confident as this one. She wouldn't be very good for protection."

"I'm still considering this one, but I'd like to see the golden."

A few minutes later the lady returns with the dog. The dog's tail thumps on the floor as she crouches to the ground. I sit on the floor. "It's alright, little one. I'll protect you."

That was it. I don't want another protection dog, even though I live alone. I want one that needs my protection. I would never be dependent on any other person or animal to keep me from harm. If I bring home another dog like Rex, I'll remain in this victim state that I've been in for far too long. I need to be the one in control of my circumstances.

The dog slowly crawls into my lap and licks my face.

"I'll take her."

I spend the next several weeks in preparation. For what, I'm not sure. I just need to be ready. Instead of going to the gun range once a week, as had been the pre-me-becoming-a-killer practice, I go every day. I shoot so many rounds with my small carry weapon that I become as accurate with it as I am with the Glock 19.

I use the person-shaped targets that Jacob had stored in our garage and rarely miss. In fact, my shots don't just hit the target, most of them are dead center. I'm not sure when or if I will ever need to use either of my guns for protection, but if I do, it will be so automatic that I won't be bogged down with uncertainty like I had been last time.

Jacob's punching bag in the garage gets more use than it ever has—just one more step in becoming strong in body and mind. It's the strengthening of my spirit that I need work on.

I've only heard from Jacob in his three-word texts that he sends every day.

Are you okay?

And every day I respond with one word.

Yes.

I probably should ask how he's doing. I just can't right now. I can't allow myself to acknowledge how worried I am about him—how much I miss him. There are just too many unanswered questions. I'm tired of waiting for Jacob to fulfill his promise of telling me everything. I have to take control of that too.

❧ ❧

Agent Stuart is waiting for me at the Double Shot during my lunch break. "I'm surprised you called me," he says as I sit across the table from him.

"Me too," I say.

"You've heard from Jacob?" he asks.

I shake my head. "That's not why I called you." The agent narrows his eyes in concentration. "There's just so much that I don't know about my husband. It's driving me crazy." I rub my forehead with my fingertips in an attempt to massage away my frustration.

"I can't give you information about an active

investigation if that's what you want," he says.

"I know," I say, sitting up in my chair and looking at him. "I'm wondering if there's anything you can share with me—something that might be available to the public—like court documents or arrest reports or something. From before, I mean."

"I'm not sure whether…"

"Please. I need to know everything I can, not just to fulfill my curiosity, but for my own safety as well."

The agent leans forward. "Is there a reason for you to feel unsafe, Katherine? Has something happened?"

I consider telling him about my meeting with Juan and Jimmy. I haven't even told Ed about it, and I'm pretty sure if I had, Ed would tell me not to tell anyone else. "No," I say. "Not specifically. But if those men, Jacob's family, want to get to him, it makes sense that they'd use me in order to do it."

Agent Stuart lets out a sigh, sits back, and crosses his arms. I think he's softening, but it could be an act. Just in case, I say. "I need to know more about the man I lived with for over three years because the man I knew could never do those awful things to anyone."

"Oh, he's capable, alright," he says. "Is there something in particular that you want to know?"

"About the human trafficking."

"Ah," Stuart says. "It's not what you think. Most people think human trafficking is only about sex slaves and drugs. The trafficking that Emilio's family was involved in is different, and Emilio's involvement with that part of the family business was limited."

"What was his involvement?" I say.

Stuart looks to the side for a moment. "I'll gather whatever appropriate paperwork I can share with you and drop it by your house later."

The outside chance of Jacob watching our house makes me hesitate. "It might be better if you drop it at my work. I'm in and out a lot and wouldn't want to miss you."

The agent nods.

"Thank you, Agent Stuart. You have no idea how much this means to me."

He nods. "There's something I've been meaning to ask you."

"Okay," I say warily.

"You said at the police station that you don't remember traveling to North Carolina last October." The agent waits for me to respond. I don't. "In our investigation, I've discovered that you and your husband stayed at the Staybridge Suites at Wrightsville Beach in North Carolina on the weekend of October nineteenth and twentieth."

I feel my face heat up, and I know that Agent Stuart knows that I'm about to lie. "Oh yeah. I forgot about that."

"You see, Katherine, the Harty brothers were murdered that weekend," he says, narrowing his eyes. "Was there any time that weekend that you weren't with your husband?"

He keeps saying your husband instead of Emilio like he had earlier. I can distance myself from Emilio, not from my husband, and he knows it. "I can't remember any time that we were apart," I lie. The truth is that Jacob had left me reading on the beach for about an hour while he went to the store and bought food to fix for dinner. Was one hour long enough for Jacob to murder two people, clean himself up, and pick up groceries? I didn't think so, but I couldn't be sure.

"Are you sure?" he asks.

My voice shakes as I answer. "As sure as I can be."

The agent stares at me for an uncomfortable amount of time and then stands. "Katherine, promise me something." He waits until I'm standing and looking at him. "Promise me that you'll let me know if you hear from Emilio or anyone else in his family."

I nod, and he leaves.

The package from Agent Stuart arrives shortly before I leave for the day. It's thicker than I'd expected, and it takes every bit of self-control I have not to rip it open. I stuff it under my passenger seat when I get into my car. I consider going straight home instead of to the range, but some part of me knows that it's best if I stick to my regular schedule. It's the only thing I have left that I can control.

I shoot poorly—well, poorly for me. No matter how hard I try, I can't achieve the calmness needed in order to hit my mark. Frustrated, I head for home.

Stella whines as I disarm the alarm. She jumps up and

down in front of me, waiting for me to acknowledge her. "It's going to be a short walk this time," I tell her. Even though the walk is only ten minutes long, it feels more like an hour. The envelope calls me.

I make a quick sandwich and grab a banana before settling down at the dining room table. The envelope contains court transcripts, notes about the investigation, newspaper clippings, and the photos of Jacob's handiwork.

The photos of the Harty brothers haunt me. I don't want to believe that Jacob had murdered those men while I sat on the beach. He certainly didn't behave suspiciously before or after the incident. Could I have married a man as coldhearted as this? If he did do it, why had he? How long had this been brewing before the night of the intrusion?

I read the whole packet. I'm left with more questions than I had before I started reading. Questions that I didn't think to ask before. It's past midnight, and I have to work in the morning. I rub my eyes and gather both of my cell phones before heading to the guest room. I have a text message on the phone Jacob gave me.

(Jacob) Are you okay?

(Me) Peachy

I plug both phones in and get ready for bed. Jacob's phone buzzes.

(Jacob) You still up?

(Me) Unfortunately

(Jacob) Can you meet?

(Me) Now?

It takes several minutes for him to respond.

(Jacob) Please?

I sigh.

(Me) Where?

(Jacob) Parking garage.

I know that I shouldn't go. Meeting Jacob would be dangerous. And stupid.

(Me) Be there shortly

❧ ❧

Jacob is waiting for me in the parking space where I'd left him the last time I saw him. He climbs in the passenger seat of my car. He looks huge, sitting in my little car. He's obviously been working out again. Looks like he's preparing for something too. At least he knows what for.

Jacob's hair has grown out a bit, his curls are wild and twisted, and his beard looks scraggly and unkempt. His clothes are worn and dirty. He looks like a homeless person—I guess he is.

"Your beard," I say.

Jacob rubs it with his hand. "You like it?"

I know he's joking, but I'm not in the joking mood. "You look like a terrorist," I say. Jacob chuckles. "It's a good disguise though; I barely recognize you." After a moment, I say, "I guess I never knew you anyway."

"You look good," Jacob says, ignoring my statement.

"Stop, Jacob. Just stop."

Jacob sighs and runs his fingers through his tangled hair. "You talked to Stuart?"

He formed it as a question, but I know it isn't. "So."

"Can I ask what you told him?"

"Why should I tell you? It's not like you've given me information that might keep me from getting killed," I say gripping the steering wheel. "It's funny how you come out of hiding because you're afraid of me telling the FBI secrets. I can't tell them anything because I don't know anything. All I know is that you lied to me. Our whole relationship has been a lie."

Jacob turns sideways in his seat and looks at me. It's dark so I can't read what he is thinking even if I could trust my judgement. "Our relationship is not a lie. You and me, it's the only part of my life that's worthy of protecting."

"Whatever."

"Katherine," he says and waits for me to look at him. He touches my hand, and I pull away. I can't trust myself not to be fooled by his gentleness. "Katherine."

I look at him. "You said you would tell me the truth. You said you would tell me everything, but I haven't heard from you in weeks."

"I check on you every day."

I chuckle sarcastically, "Three-word texts."

"You think I want to stay away from you?" he says. "It's driving me crazy. But I have to stay away to protect you."

"Protect me from what?" I snap. He doesn't answer. "How can I possibly protect myself if I don't know what's out there?"

His voice is quiet when he says, "I'm so sorry." I have to look away. "Will you please tell me why Agent Stuart wanted to talk to you?"

Still staring out the windshield, I say, "I called him."

Out of the corner of my eye, I see Jacob flinch. "Why?"

I look at him. "I have so many questions. I need to— no, I deserve to know the answers."

"So, you asked Stuart?" He sounds incredulous.

"It wasn't like there was anyone else to ask."

Jacob rubs his beard. "Was he able to give you the answers you're looking for?"

"Some," I say. "He gave me a packet of information from before. He couldn't tell me anything they've found out in their current investigation of you."

He sits up and turns more toward me. "Ask me anything, and I'll answer if I can. I promise."

If I can. I hesitate, trying to decide what to ask first. I decide to start with an easy one. "When I was being questioned by the police, they mentioned that your family was into human trafficking."

"They did?" he asks.

I nod.

"They're probably talking about my uncle. Julio owned a cleaning company that had contracts with high-end hotels in Florida and Georgia. I don't know if you know this, but companies can petition the government to allow them to bring workers from other countries."

I shake my head.

"So, Julio would inflate the number of workers that he needed, and once he got approved for a certain number of workers, he'd send someone or hire someone from the country he's getting workers from, South America or eastern Europe mostly. This person would recruit workers, promising them more money than they'd ever made before, which is pretty attractive. Most planned to send a large percentage of their salary home.

"But when they get here, they aren't paid what they were promised. Most can't speak English, so they're dependent on my uncle's company for everything. The company would provide transportation to work or to the store for a fee. Julio would pay them minimum wage but then subtract a transportation fee or housing fee. The workers maybe make two dollars an hour if they're lucky."

Jacob sighs. "When a worker's visa runs out, Julio would charge them an exorbitant amount to travel home—more money than they could possibly save, so they're stuck here illegally, which gives Julio even more leverage."

"Shit," I say.

"That's why they sent me after Antonio," Jacob says,

146

running his hands through his hair.

"Your cousin?"

Jacob's eyes widen. "They told you that?" I nod. "Antonio was secretly helping people get back to their home countries."

"So, when they found out…"

"They sent me," he says. "My family had this cabin that was perfect for this kind of thing." He shrugs. "No neighbors." He stares out the windshield and continues. "I had no idea who I was going to see when I walked into the room. That wasn't unusual. What was unusual was that my brothers insisted to go with me."

Jacob squeezes his eyes shut and shakes his head before resuming his staring. "When I saw Antonio strapped to the chair, I refused to—you know, to rough him up. He was family, and you don't turn on your family. I should've untied him and let him leave, but I just left." He looks at me. "I hate myself for leaving him there. I thought they would just…"

"Rough him up?" I ask.

Jacob nods. "I didn't know," he sobs. "I didn't know they were going to kill him. Antonio was closer than a brother to me, and I didn't do anything to protect him."

My hand lifts slightly. I want to reach out and comfort him, but I can't risk it. I nod, encouraging him to go on.

"Everything changed in me after that. That's when I decided to betray my own family. For Antonio."

"I'm sorry, Jacob."

He grabs my hand. "I'm not proud of my past, Katherine. I never wanted you to know who—what I truly am."

We sit in silence for several minutes, Jacob holding my hand while I try to decide whether I should pull it away. I need to go home and get some sleep if I can. But after reading the packet the agent gave me and seeing Jacob, I doubt I'll be able to sleep anyway. I pull my hand free and say, "I need to go, Jacob, but I have to ask you one more question."

"Okay."

I pulled out the picture from the Harty brothers' murder crime scene. "Did you do this?"

"No."

"They think you did. It happened the same weekend we went to Wrightsville Beach."

"I didn't kill them."

I want to believe him, but it was just too coincidental. "How can you explain it then? Were you afraid that they would tell your family where to find you? I mean, look at their thumbs, Jacob. It's your signature."

"No," Jacob says firmly. "I didn't do it, Katherine, I swear."

"Then who did?"

"I don't know exactly who, but whoever it was, was sent by my family."

"But how?"

Jacob leans in closer to me. "I think they've been watching me for a long time. I didn't notice. I let myself get too comfortable in my new life." He leans toward me. "And it cost you. I will never forgive myself for that."

"You said that you didn't kill the Hardy brothers, but you have killed before, haven't you?"

"You know that I have," he says.

"I don't mean the men who broke into our house, I mean before."

Jacob looks away. "It was a long time ago."

"How many?"

"Please, Katherine. It's not something I want to talk about—not just because I don't want you to know but because I don't want to relive it. I was a different man then."

"What now, Jacob?"

"I have a plan," he says.

"Plan?"

"It's complicated and best if you don't know what it is."

"Jacob."

"I'm serious, Katherine. It's safer for both of us if you don't know."

I sigh. "I hate secrets."

"I know," he says gently. "I wish I didn't have to keep anything from you but…"

"It's safer," I say sarcastically.

"You look exhausted. You should get at least a little sleep."

Why does asking questions only lead to more questions? I wish I could run like I had before. I wish that would be enough this time, but I know it can't be. Never again. "When can I know this plan, Jacob?"

"Soon," he says, whatever that means. I know I will get no more answers from Jacob tonight.

"Can I drop you somewhere."

Jacob shakes his head. "It's best if…"

"I don't know where you're staying," I finish for him.

"I'm sorry, Katherine."

I nod.

Jacob gets out of the car, but before he shuts the door, he leans in and says, "I love you."

I close my eyes tight. Without looking at him, I say, "Be safe, Jacob."

He nods, shuts the door, and disappears into the darkness.

It's only been two weeks since I'd last seen my father, but he looks like it's been much longer. The guard supports the reverend under the elbow as he shuffles into the room. He's smaller today, not just in physical size but in his demeanor, as if he has no fight left in him—as if he has nothing left to live for. Did I do this to him?

The guard takes off the reverend's chains and helps him into his seat. Before turning to leave, the guard gives me a warning look. I smile weakly at him, trying to convey that I have no intention of inflicting injury on my father today. He doesn't return the smile.

"Thank you for coming," the reverend says.

Seeing this withered man in front of me, the man who was my hero when I was a girl, the man whom I vowed to hate forever, breaks something inside me. He may be the monster who murdered my mother. But he is also the man who carried me on his shoulders—the man who patiently taught me to drive—the man who comforted me after my first break up—the one who told me that not all boys were stupid and that one day I'd find one who realized how precious and special I am and would refuse to let me go. Like Jacob.

As ridiculous as it sounds, I can understand his actions. Admittedly, his reasons for murdering my mother are terrible, unjustifiable, and inadequate. But I understand all that he feared losing. Ironically, he lost much more than he'd been trying to protect. I can't begin to imagine what that must be like for him. I told myself that I didn't care. But that was a lie.

So many lies. Why does there have to be so many lies? Part of me wants to protect myself and not reveal the depth of my emotion—to just apologize and get out before I let myself be vulnerable before the man who shattered me—the man whom I shattered the last time we were in this room. There's been too much of that. Life is painful sometimes, and love, well, I'm finding that it's painful most of the time.

"Dad," my voice breaks, and I start to cry. "Dad, I'm so sorry about—"

The reverend reaches for my hand and gently squeezes it. "I know, Kate. I know."

We sit in silence. I look at my hand in his and remember when my hand was so small, I could only grip a couple of his fingers as we walked across the street to the church. Now his hand is the one that looks small, and I know that this will be the last time these two hands will be together.

"Do you remember Spot the Miracle?" His voice is gentle.

"Yeah," I say and look into his blue eyes. Those were the eyes that used to represent pure love to me. As hard as I try, I can't make them the eyes of a murderer. They're the eyes of a father who loves his daughter.

"Well," he says and gestures toward our clasped hands. "I can see one right now." A couple tears escape his eyes, and he wipes them away with his free hand. He nods toward the rosary clasped tightly in my other hand. "That would really please your mother."

I stiffen for a moment, a little irritated that he would bring her up. But of course, he would. He doesn't have time to run from the truth anymore. "I miss her so much, Dad," I sob.

"I know you do, Kate, and I'm so sorry," he says. "Believe it or not, I miss her too."

I believe him. I know how difficult it was for me to cope with how I treated him the last time, even if I was a little justified. The guilt of it ate me up inside. Words can't be unsaid, and my mother can't be brought back no matter how much we want it to be so. I can't imagine how he's lived with his guilt. It has to be far worse than the cancer that's killing him.

Something deep inside me tries to remind me that I'm supposed to hate him, but this time I ignore it. Hating him hasn't helped me cope with my mother's death and certainly hasn't been healthy for me. It has to end now, for my sake and for his. He should be able to go to the grave remembering this moment. Let God be the judge of what happens to him after he dies.

We speak of little things, of pleasant memories and hopes for what comes next. I don't tell him about the chaos of my life with Jacob, and he doesn't tell me of his life in prison or whether he fears death. We just sit in each other's presence for the thirty-minute allotted time for our visit. It's both healing and heartbreaking.

The door opens and the guard says, "Time's up, Reverend." I'm not ready. I know that this is the last time I'll see this man alive; he obviously doesn't have much time left. I squeeze his hand. He grips mine tightly before slipping his hand from mine.

The reverend stands, allowing the guard to place the chains back on and help him toward the door. I'm still sitting; I can't seem to move. As the reverend gets to the door, I say, "I forgive you, Dad." And I mean it.

The reverend sobs. "I love you, Kate."

"I love you too," I say automatically.

I have come to realize that love is irrational. How can I love the man who killed my mother? I can't explain it—I don't want to love him, but I do.

He's my father.

I add one thing to my daily routine: investigating Jacob. I read the agent's packet so many times that I've almost memorized it. I conduct internet searches on the Vaquez family, money laundering, identity theft, and loan sharking, anything that will help me predict what Jacob is up to. But no amount of reading will help me think like Jacob. I can't think like Jacob because I'm not like Jacob.

And that thought terrifies me.

It terrifies me because it amplifies the fact that I don't know my husband. I never did. But that doesn't mean that I didn't love him. I still do. I wish I didn't. Then I could move on with my life. I can't do that because, even though Jacob is a mystery to me, he is my life. Is there anything more pathetic than that?

I have to find a way to look at all of this without my feelings getting involved. I need to look at this logically and intelligently. I need to stop thinking of my husband as Jacob Varga and start recognizing who he actually is: Emilio Vasquez, the son of Enrique, the brother to Juan and EJ, the one who beat people when they owed his family money, the one who broke thumbs.

The one who informed on his own family, the one who started a new life, the one I fell in love with. No. That's Jacob, and Jacob is not Emilio.

But Jacob is Emilio, and Emilio is Jacob, just like the reverend is both my father that loves me and the monster that murdered my mother. I'd forgiven the reverend that day when I'd visited him in jail. I'd meant it, but I'm finding that I will have to forgive him many times before it actually sticks. Maybe it's the same with Jacob. But first I'll have to accept that everything that has happened to us, to me, the past couple months is not something that Jacob planned or instigated to hurt me or to make me unsafe. He didn't want me to be a victim any more than the reverend wanted me to be one. I can either remain a victim or choose to take control and survive. I need to start working with Jacob instead of against him because if I'm going to survive all of this, I need both the Jacob and Emilio sides of my husband. Now I just need to convince him that he needs me too.

I'm so tired. I lie on the bed, still fully dressed, with my two phones resting on my chest. I close my eyes just for a minute when my cell phone vibrates. I grab it quickly and read the message.

You up?

My heart leaps. Jacob probably wants me to come to another middle of the night meeting. I want to see Jacob in person, but I don't know if it's wise. It's been weeks since I last spoke to him in person. I need to see him.

(Me) Yes.

As I press send on my message, I realize that this is not the phone that Jacob had given me. It's my personal phone. I sit bolt upright and stare at the phone.

I answer the phone on the first ring. "Hello."

"Katherine, it's Luke." My heart drops, not just because it's my brother on the other end of the line instead of my husband, but because I'm pretty sure I know what he's going to say next. "I'm sorry to call you so late," Luke says.

"He's dead, isn't he," I say.

"Yes," Luke whispers.

The news crashes into me like ice cold water, clearing my head of the sleepiness that had been fogging it. "When?"

Luke sighs. "A couple hours ago. I just left the prison."

"I didn't know he'd gotten worse," I say trying to hide the hurt in my voice from feeling left out. Why didn't Luke call me? A better question might be, "Why should he call me?" I haven't been our father's biggest fan. It's just that I thought since I'd visited the reverend and sort of made peace with him, that I might have earned the right to be informed if he was actually dying.

"It was fast," Luke said. "You wouldn't have made it. I didn't even get there in time, and I left the house as soon as they called." His voice breaks, and I can hear him crying.

I should be crying. I've just been informed that my father is dead, so I should be crying. But I can't. I'm not sure how I feel about it. Part of me is saying, "It's about time," but the other part wishes that I had more time to— to what? Fix our relationship? When your father murders your mother, it doesn't leave much room for familial relationship.

What should I be feeling? What am I feeling? I can't name it. It's not sadness, not about the reverend being dead. At least, I don't think so. It's deeper. It's more as if my very self is being reformed by the news. I'm not sure what to say to Luke right now. So, I settle for simply, "Okay."

"I'll call the funeral home tomorrow to make the arrangements," Luke says.

"Okay."

"Do you want to be there?"

"Um," I say. "I'm not sure if I can." I don't need to

elaborate. My brother knows me well enough to know that I can't enter the same funeral home that handled the arrangements for our mother's funeral and make arrangements for the man who murdered her. I'm not sure how Luke can. He's a better person than me and a whole lot better at forgiving.

"Okay," he says. "Just thought I'd ask."

"Luke, I'll come if you need me to."

"It's okay, Sis," he says gently. "I have Lori this time."

He might as well have kicked me in the stomach. "I'm sorry."

"I love you, Katherine."

"I love you too, Luke," I say. "Thank you for…" I'm not sure how to finish that sentence.

"I'll call you with the funeral arrangements when they're finished."

"Okay."

"You'll come, won't you?" Luke asks.

"I'll try," I say.

"That's all I ask," he says and disconnects the call.

I want to call Jacob. I hold the cell phone Jacob gave me and stare at it, trying to decide whether to push the button. I miss my husband, and truthfully, I've never needed him more than I do at this moment. But I can't push the button. I can't keep looking to Jacob to make me strong. I have to be strong on my own; the next few days will require it.

I can't convince myself to go in. I've been sitting in my car in front of the church that I'd grown up considering a second home for over an hour. The service would've begun ten minutes ago. But I couldn't do it. The last time I'd been here was to attend my mother's funeral—a funeral presided over by my father.

I know I should go in there if only to support Luke. My hand on the door handle, I will myself to pull, but I can't bring myself to. I remove my hand and notice it shaking vigorously. In fact, everything inside me vibrates like a jackhammer. Tears threaten, not for the loss of my father, but for the memory of first finding my dead mother and then saying a final goodbye to her here. The weight of her loss is overwhelming today. It's as if my heart weighs five hundred pounds as it rests on my stomach. It's all just too much for me to handle.

I start my car, intending to leave, but a small voice inside my head somehow makes itself heard amidst all of the hammering. This isn't about you. I turn off my car and pull the handle. A tingling in the back of my neck stops me. Looking down the street in both directions, all is still. I reach down to my ankle and feel my gun resting beneath the black slacks I wore. I pull the gun and get out. Holding the gun beside my leg, I turn and strain to see as far as I can but see nothing out of the ordinary. Will I ever get rid of this paranoia? Instead of returning the gun to my ankle holster, I tuck it the back of my waistband. It's heavy, and I fear it will fall out if I move too much.

I'm leaning against the front of my car as people begin exiting the church. I'm taken aback when I see Jordan standing just inside the door, shaking hands as the funeral attendants leave. Of course, he'd be here. He's the new pastor. I don't know why I didn't consider it before, but he must've presided over the ceremony. This was going to get awkward.

I wave at Luke when he appears, and he gestures toward the limousine that was to take the family to the cemetery. I shake my head. I'm not quite ready to face everyone yet. I climb into my car, remove the gun from my waist band, and return it to its holster. As the procession leaves, I pull my car behind the row of cars.

I'm shocked and a little disappointed that so many

have shown up today. It feels as if my mother is victimized once again by this. It looks like less than half the number of people that were at her service, but still way more than the reverend deserves.

It's not about you.

It's true. It's not about me. Perhaps, it's not about the reverend either. It's possible that these people are here to support Luke. Isn't that why I came? I ask myself but refuse to ponder the answer.

Again, I look all around me before exiting the car. Surely, whoever is out there won't do anything with all these people around. If anyone is out there.

I walk behind the other mourners to my father's graveside. I'm relieved to see that he will not be buried next to my mother as was planned years ago. We'd even bought a double headstone for them. That was when I still believed the reverend was innocent. I'm so grateful that Luke had decided that Mom should be able to rest in peace without her killer next to her. It was just one of the many decisions that he'd had to make without me this week. My stomach clenches. I deserve all the guilty feelings that I have for not being here for him.

The people in front of me part and look at me, and I realize that they are clearing a path for me to sit with Luke by the gravesite. I hesitate but force myself to move forward. Luke grabs my hand as I sit next to him, and I lay my head on his shoulder. "I'm sorry for not sitting with you earlier."

He kisses the top of my head and says, "You're here now." How could I have abandoned my sweet brother for so long?

Jordan smiles weakly at me as he makes his way in front of us. I look in the direction of my mother's grave and try my best not to listen to his prayers for the reverend's soul. It's not that I want my father condemned to hell. Not really. There was a time that I prayed for that. It's what he deserved.

However, if he deserved damnation for taking my mother's life, what about Jacob? What about me? Hadn't we taken lives as well? Sure, circumstances were very different between them. Maybe Jacob and I were justified in what we'd done on the night of the invasion. Nonetheless, our actions left mothers without sons and children without fathers, just as the reverend's left Luke and me motherless.

I glance at my brother and pray that someday I'll be able to show some of God's mercy and fully forgive our father as he had. Luke is a much better person than me. I used to be better. Maybe one day I can be again.

Once the prayer is over, Luke leans in and says, "There will be a lunch reception at my house after we leave here."

"It's not at the church?" I ask.

"No," he said. "I figured that would be difficult for you."

I'd planned on leaving for Charleston when this was over, so I wouldn't have to enter the church property. Part of me still wants to, but I know I can't. I can't abandon Luke any more than I have already. "Yeah," I say. "Thank you."

Luke turns to shake someone's hand, and after pulling a few carnations out of one of the reverend's flower arrangements, I slip away. No one stops me as I walk to my mother's grave. I haven't been here since the day of the reverend's sentencing over five years ago.

The double headstone still sits at my mother's head. I have a strong urge to get the crowbar out of my car and destroy the marker. I probably wouldn't be able to break it, but I might be able to scratch my father's name out.

I'm pelted with conflicting emotions. I'm still angry at my father; that's for sure. But not as angry as I once was. I can even admit that I love the man. There was a time I believed that was an impossibility. Part of me still hates him; however, that part is smaller, too.

Kneeling in the grass, I place the flowers in the vase attached to my mother's side of the marker. I trace my mother's name with my finger over and over. Anna Lynn Baker. "I could use your advice right now, Mom." I speak the words quietly. "God, I miss you."

My eyes well up, but no tears fall. I'm not sure how I manage it. How can I be so strong in some areas and so weak in others? It's like I'm two different people, both of them warring for control. I've ignored half of myself for most of my life. Now, I need that side the most if I'm to survive what's coming, whatever that is.

Something moves to my left in the distance. I raise my knee and place my foot on the ground as if I were getting up. I slide my Glock 42 out and stand with the gun resting next to my leg. Turning around and around, trying to make out what had moved. Nothing.

I've pulled my gun today more than I ever have. My emotions have me on high alert. I wish I would've worn my belly band holster. I'd chosen the ankle holster today because I was afraid someone might feel it when I hugged them. Now, I'm wishing I would've found a way to keep from hugging people instead of carrying my gun where it was difficult to access.

I return my gun to its holster and head for Luke's house. So focused on making sure I'm not being followed, I hardly notice my hometown as I make my way to Luke's, which is probably a good thing. I'm not ready to relive the memories that I've been repressing. There was a time when I knew the names of the people living in almost every house here—people that I haven't let myself think about—people that I hurt when I left. I hadn't realized until this moment how selfish my running away had been.

Leaning against the wall of the hallway and watching the guests interact in the living room, I feel like an outsider. Once, I would've been in the middle of these people, these friends, and asking if I could get them anything. Now, I'm an outsider looking into my old life, a life that could've been mine, if only…

I'd said hello to the people in the living room when I'd first arrived, but I hadn't lingered. It wasn't that they didn't welcome me; it was more that I deflected their welcome with an invisible wall of protection. I can't let myself be vulnerable anywhere, especially here where my mother's memory lurks in every person who had meant so much to her. It's all about survival at this point. I can revisit demons from my past in Harrison after the danger from the Vasquez family is behind me.

The women in the room in front of me try to be subtle in their glances at me. I attempt to smile politely, but I'm afraid I'm failing to look sincere. Which one, if any, will have the courage to approach me to find out where I've been all this time? It won't matter who; if one of them is brave enough to ask, they'll all know every detail before the day is out.

A baby with a pink ruffled dress and pink bows in her stubby pigtails crawls out of the crowd toward me. She gets caught on her dress a couple times before she lifts her knees and crawls on her hands and feet instead. Crawling with a purpose, she reaches me and puts her hand on my shin so she can pull herself up. Moving my gun leg back, I bend to pick her up. "Well, hello there," I say smiling wide.

At first, she returns the smile, but then she pokes out her bottom lip, wrinkles her face, and lets out the saddest, cutest cry ever. "Oh, it's okay, Sweetie," I say, patting her back and bouncing up and down.

Jordan approaches from the kitchen. "It's alright, Esther," he says, patting the baby on the back. "Katherine isn't as scary as she looks standing here by herself."

I chuckle. "Thanks. But if you ask them," I say gesturing to the women in the living room, "I'm terrifying."

He smiles. "Maybe it's the way you're standing or the expression on your face, daring someone to get past your

Perron

guard."

"You're not afraid."

"Terrified," he said winking. "I just came to rescue my daughter."

I hand the baby over. "She's beautiful."

"That she is," Jordan says. "She takes after her mother."

The silence that follows is interrupted by Luke. Handing me a glass of iced tea, he says, "You look thirsty." I smile and nod.

"How've you been, Katherine?" Jordan asks.

"Fine," I say bringing on more awkward silence.

Luke breaks the quiet. "I was hoping to meet—um—your husband."

"Jacob," I say smiling. "He couldn't get away."

"Not even to come to your father's funeral?" Luke asks.

I narrow my eyes. "I wasn't that close to the reverend," I say, making my stomach clinch. "He would've been here if there was any way he could." If he wasn't hiding.

Luke shook his head in disapproval. Family is everything in a small town, and there's no way that any man from here would make his wife go to any funeral alone, especially if it was her father's. "I'm going to get something to eat. Can I get you anything?"

"Cake," I say.

168

"Of course," he says, knowing that cake has always been my favorite.

I think that Jordan will take this opportunity to leave, but he asks, "So, what does he do?"

"Jacob?" I ask, biding time to think of an answer.

"Jacob. Yes," he says.

I smile wide, hoping it doesn't look forced. "If I told you, I'd have to kill you." We laugh politely. "No, really," I say. "It's boring stuff involving difficult math for important people. I don't understand it, no matter how many times he's tried to explain it to me."

"Are you teaching?" Jordan asks.

I'd talked about becoming an elementary school teacher for most of my childhood. My best friend Melanie and I were going to have adjoining classrooms at Harrison Elementary. I shake my head. "I'm actually a legal secretary for a prominent defense attorney in Charleston."

Jordan knit his brow. "But you always dreamed..."

"A lot of my dreams died when—when I left Harrison," I say meeting his eyes. "Enough about me. Tell me about you."

He smiled. "Well, Beth and I have been married for almost four years. We have a three-year-old son named Ethan, who's running around here somewhere, probably close to the food. I took over as pastor of the church a few years ago, as I'm sure you know." He doesn't tell me that he and his family now live in the house that I grew up in— the house that we thought one day we would live in to raise our family.

"I'm happy for you, Jordan," I say. "I'm so glad that my leaving hadn't…"

"It gutted me," he said. "I met Beth shortly after forcing myself to go back to school. I didn't want to return to the seminary. My faith was—let's just say that it had been tested. I wasn't sure I could ever regain…We were just friends for a while. She helped me through the worst of it and then we became more."

"Jordan," a woman's voice coming from the kitchen. "Ethan needs you in the bathroom."

"Well, it was good catching up," I say.

"Katherine," he says, "don't ever settle for less than you deserve."

I smile. "Take care of that family of yours." As I watch him leave, I wonder what it would've been like if I'd stayed. Would I be the one married to Jordan? Would I have kids? If I'd stayed, I wouldn't have met Jacob. I wouldn't have killed nor would I be so paranoid that I'm constantly being followed—being pursued. I wouldn't be in danger. My life would've been so much simpler if only I would've stayed.

No! I'm surprised by the forcefulness of my thought. I have many regrets, but not marrying Jordan isn't one of them. Neither was marrying Jacob, despite the consequences of it.

I sit with Luke on the couch to eat my cake, which must have made approaching me less intimidating. Everyone I spoke with welcomed me with kindness and love, which is probably what I'd been afraid of. It's difficult to deny the guilt I feel over leaving when I'm faced with such charity.

Lori hugs me tightly when I leave, and Luke walks me to my car. It feels as if all the air leaves my body when I reach my car. My breath catches when I see it. Stuck under the windshield wiper on the driver's side is a single white carnation.

"You must have an admirer," Luke says.

I force a smile. "Maybe so." I hold Luke for several minutes, just trying to steady myself enough to drive. "I'm sorry that you've had to take care of so much alone."

"Don't stay away so long this time, okay?"

"Keep me posted about the baby," I say.

"You'll be my first phone call."

I grab the flower and get in the car. I roll down my window. "I love you, Luke."

"I love you too, Kate," he says, leaning in to kiss me on the cheek. "Bring the husband next time."

I nod, knowing that the likelihood of that was almost nil.

I drive home paying as much attention to my review mirror as I do the road. Someone must be following me, but I can't pinpoint which one of the cars behind me is the one. This is all so frustrating. I just want to slam on my breaks, climb out of my car and scream "What the hell do you want?"

I'm exhausted by the time I pick Stella up from the kennel and make it to my house. I go straight to bed. I'm not sure I'll be able to sleep with my stomach in knots both from being followed and from the emotions from the day. I feel like I need a good cry, but so far, I haven't shed a single tear since my dad died. I can't let myself be vulnerable right now.

When I'd told the reverend that I forgave him for murdering my mother, I'd meant it. Today reminded me that I haven't fully let go of my hatred for him. I love him but hate him at the same time. Maybe by the time I leave this world myself, I'll somehow be free of this anger. It certainly doesn't help that I love a man that is just as untrustworthy as my father. I want to trust Jacob. I want to love him without obstacles. Unfortunately, in order to do that, I'd have to pretend the last few months had never happened. It takes so much time and effort to build trust but only a moment to destroy it. I'm not sure that Jacob and I can make it back to the place we were before I knew his secrets.

I lie in bed, reading but not focusing, staring at the ceiling but not seeing, feeling miserable but having no tears to release my agony. I'm lonely, and I can't imagine there ever being a possibility for me to not be. My skin aches to be touched. I rub my arms vigorously, trying to stop the tingling. I close my eyes and pray that I can sleep, so I can escape this emptiness for at least a few hours.

Stella can't get comfortable either. She keeps walking in circles on the bed, trying to find a place where she can rest. She's probably having trouble finding a spot because of me and my anxiety. I grab Stella and pull her close to me. I stroke her fur until she begins to relax. This simple gesture defuses some of my loneliness, and I start to drift.

Stella jerks upright and lets out a screeching bark. "I hear it too," I tell her and jump out of bed to grab my Glock 19. I crouch behind the bed as the beeping of my home security system stops.

Someone is in my house.

Stella shakes violently and lets out a long high-pitched whine. "Hush," I tell her, straining to hear what's going on outside the room. I ready the gun and carefully take aim at what would be chest high of the intruder. "Please, God. Don't make me have to kill again."

A soft knock at the bedroom door sends Stella into a frenzy of barking.

"It's me," Jacob says, and I let out the breath I'm holding.

As I unlock the bedroom door, I say, "Geez, Jacob. I almost shot you."

He smiles wide, "You did?" The pride in his voice can't be mistaken. Jacob gestures to the gun that I'm holding at my side. "That's an improvement."

"Home protection doesn't need to be fashionable."

Jacob looks at Stella cowering behind the bed. "I think your dog is defective."

"It's okay, Stella," I say. She crawls low to the ground before rolling to her back in front of Jacob.

Jacob pats her and says, "Some guard dog you are."

I walk to the other side of the bed and return my gun to its case. "Why are you here, Jacob?"

His eyes grow gentle. "I knew your dad's funeral was today and that you went home for it. I just wanted to check on you."

"How did you know—wait, you were there weren't you?"

"Where?"

"You followed me to Harrison, didn't you?"

Jacob's brow furrowed. "No."

"Are you sure, Jacob? Because I was sure that someone was watching me."

"That wasn't me," Jacob said softly. "What exactly did you see?"

I shake my head, not sure whether to believe him. "It doesn't matter."

"Are you okay?"

"Of course; I'm always okay," I say, but the quiver in my voice betrays me.

Jacob closes the distance between us and pulls me into his arms. I resist at first, but the warmth of him is so inviting and so familiar, I pull him tight against me. Inhaling deeply, I close my eyes and bask in his scent and let myself melt into him. It's funny how we just fit together—like two pieces in the same puzzle—both worn and frayed at the edges but still click together despite all that tries to hold us apart.

Several minutes pass in silence. Words are not needed to convey all that needs to be communicated. For a moment, I try to remind myself that Jacob isn't trustworthy, that he's not the man I thought he was, and that I'm still angry at him, but the tender way he holds me and gently rubs my back tells me that he's still the Jacob I know—the Jacob I love. Am I naïve to ignore everything that I've discovered, or failed to discover, about my husband and cling to the hope of us being us again?

I'm pretty sure the answer to that question is yes, so I pry myself out of his arms and sit on the edge of the bed. Jacob sits next to me, close but not touching. I press my hands together as if I'm praying and bounce my fingers against my lips. Careful, Katherine. "Did I tell you that I'm going to be an aunt?" I ask.

"Really?"

"Yeah, Luke's going to have a baby just after the first of the year. Well, Luke's not. His wife Lori is."

Jacob's smile doesn't hide the sadness. "I'm glad you got to finally see your family."

My family. I don't have much of a family left. Somehow becoming parentless has left me feeling like a frightened little girl who has no idea how she's going to make it in the world without her mommy and daddy. I know it's silly. I've been on my own since the reverend's sentencing. I'd told the court that I considered myself orphaned because the man who murdered my mother could no longer be called my father. But the little girl deep inside me knew that as long as he lived, she wasn't really an orphan. Now she is.

Now I am.

I shrug my shoulders. "I saw Jordan too."

"Jordan?"

"My ex-fiancé."

Jacob raises an eyebrow. "You were engaged?"

Stella stops pacing and starts to climb on the bed. I push her off. Without looking up, I nod. Jacob doesn't say anything. "I guess we both have secrets from our lives before."

"Yeah," Jacob says. "I guess we do."

"You must think I'm a hypocrite for being so angry at you. Calling you a liar. When I left Harrison, I promised myself that I was leaving for good. I was starting over completely, and under no circumstances would I ever think or speak about my past again. I didn't see it as lying to you." I take the chance and look him in the eye. "I guess that's what you were doing too."

I know that Jacob is weighing his next words carefully. His eyes can't hide the depth of his emotion. "It's not the same."

"It is, Jacob. I'm sorry."

"No," he says firmly. "It's not. You didn't want to think about your past, so you didn't tell me about it. I didn't tell you about mine because I was ashamed of it."

"So was I."

Jacob shakes his head. "You were ashamed of what your father did. I was ashamed of what I did. You hid a fiancé; I hid my criminal background." He runs his hands through his hair. "I am so sorry that I've dragged you into what I so wanted to protect you from."

I want to say something reassuring. I want to forgive this man for everything. I want to trust him again. The trouble is that I'm not sure that I can. Not in a way that will last because there is still so much that I don't know. There is still so much that I'm afraid to know.

"How was it?" Jacob asks. "Seeing Jordan again?"

"Different." I say. "He's married now. Has two kids."

Jacob touches my cheek and says, "That could've been you."

"No. I could never be happy with him. I thought I loved him, and my mom was so excited to be planning my wedding. But truthfully, I would never make a good preacher's wife."

"He's a preacher?"

I chuckle. "Actually, he's the new pastor at the church I grew up in."

"Really?"

My eyes well up. "He presided over the reverend's funeral today. Not that I witnessed it. I couldn't bring myself to enter the place where my mom had been murdered. I just sat in my car until everyone headed to the cemetery."

Jacob takes my hand. "I'm sure that must've been difficult. I'm sorry that you went through that alone."

I shrug. "I wasn't sure that I would go at all. But I guess I'm glad I did."

"You must've missed everyone when you first left Harrison."

"Actually, I couldn't." I say. "I couldn't feel much of

179

anything back then except contempt for my father and anger toward Jordan and Luke for taking his side. I left with no intention of giving them any more of my energy.

"After a few months in Charleston, I stopped feeling altogether. I went to work, did my job, and came home alone. I guess I stopped living for a while."

"I didn't know that," Jacob says.

"I stopped feeling—until you. You woke me up, I guess, and my life started again."

"Well, I didn't live at all until you. Not my own life anyway."

"What do you mean?"

He doesn't answer at first, so I wait. He stares past me as if he sees his past in the distance. "I've done terrible things. But, you know that already." Jacob shrugs and raises the corner of his mouth in a half smile. "When I worked with Stuart, I was careful not to reveal the depth of my part in the family business. He knew it. It was part of our unspoken deal. He wouldn't ask about the people I killed, and I wouldn't incriminate myself."

He sighs and shakes his head. "You know the first time I killed someone it was an accident? I was working this guy over and went too far. It messed me up.

"My brothers were proud of me. They took me out drinking to celebrate as if killing someone was a coming-of-age thing." He shrugs. "I never had a stomach for all the violence that I was supposedly born to inflict. But I did it because it was for the family. The family. What a joke." He shakes his head. "You're my family now. My only family—

the one worth fighting for, even if I have to inflict harm on those who threaten it."

Jacob brushes the hair from my face. "You look exhausted." He stands and pulls the covers back for me to crawl in bed.

"I'm not ready to be alone yet."

"It's okay. I'll stay with you until you fall asleep."

When I crawl under the covers, Stella starts climbing on the bed again. "Stella, no."

"You don't let that dog sleep in your bed do you?"

"Maybe," I say. "I can't stand sleeping by myself anymore." I grab his hand. "Lie here with me for a while."

Jacob takes his shoes off and lies on the covers next to me. He slides his arm under me and pulls my back against his chest, and I think *this is home.*

"You really need to start sleeping in our bedroom. This bed is too small."

I swallow hard and murmur, "I can't." I shake my head. "I can't get the picture of Victor's staring eyes out of my head. I can't even go in that room."

Jacob is quiet at first, drawing circles on my arm with his fingertips. "I know it's hard. Just remember that you didn't do anything wrong."

"I killed him, Jacob. I took a father away from his kids. How can I get past that?"

Jacob tightens his arms around me. "Victor is the one who broke into our home. He's the one who tried to kill me and threatened you. You did what you had to do. His kids are fatherless because of him, not you."

I squeeze my eyes shut. "My head knows that, but—"

Jacob takes in a noisy breath and sighs it out. "I never wanted you to be a part of this—never wanted you to be faced with that impossible choice." His guilt is palpable; his regret seems larger than this room, and there's nothing to be said except I forgive you, but the words won't leave my lips.

Several seconds go by. He kisses me just below my ear, sending shivers all over my body. "When you're ready, I know you can face that room. It doesn't look much the same anyway now that the carpet is gone, and it's been repainted."

I nod. "Can we stop talking about it now?"

"Sure."

My insides quiver, and I wonder Jacob can feel it. I'm afraid, that much I know, but I'm not sure if it's from the thought of Jacob leaving me here alone or if it's from my inability to make him leave. My heart isn't safe where Jacob is concerned; it outweighs my head by a lot. I need something to ground me—to quail my quacking insides. My grandmother's rosary sits on my bedside table, and I can't resist the urge to pick it up. I put it in Jacob's hand and say, "Show me how to do this."

"Do what?" he asks. "Say the Rosary?"

"Yes," I say. "I want to know why it was so important to my mom and grandmother."

"I don't know if I remember how."

"Please," I say.

Jacob places the rosary in my hand, wrapping his hands around mine to show me how to work the beads. "We start at the crucifix," he says.

Jacob's voice is soft and deep as he recites the prayers. The rhythm of the repeated prayers, the feeling of his breath on my neck, soothe my unrest and replace it with the feeling of safety. The reverend always said that memorized prayer wasn't really prayer. Prayer to him was a conversation with God. If you weren't using your own words, it wasn't conversation. This was one thing about the reverend that I'd never doubted.

Until now. Maybe it's our closeness to each other or my raw vulnerability after a long, emotional day, but I can't remember a time when I felt this much peace. It's the most prayerful experience that I've had since I was a teenager. When the prayer is over, we remain still—just listening.

"Thank you," I say.

Jacob's arms tighten around me. "Do you know when I knew that I was in love with you?" I shake my head. "I was pretty sure that I loved you before this point, but this event sealed it for me."

"What event."

He chuckles, and his breath tickles my ear. "That Halloween when you made chili in the pumpkin."

"What? That was terrible," I say. "How did that make you fall in love with me?"

"It was your laugh," he says. "After you spat your mouthful out in the sink, you bent over laughing."

"I couldn't catch my breath."

"Neither could I. We laughed until we cried, and I knew that I couldn't live without you. Ever."

I'm stunned into silence.

"Do you know when I knew that you loved me?" he says softly.

I shake my head.

His voice drops to a whisper. "It was when you first let me call you Katie." I hold my breath because I can hear the emotion in his voice. "Katherine is for people that you hold at a distance. They're not safe. But Katie—Katie is for those you let inside your walls."

He's right. My family used to call me Kate once in a while, but they were the only ones who got away with it. No one ever called me anything but Katherine. Not even Jordan.

Only Jacob was allowed call me Katie.

"Wow," I say. "I never knew that."

Jacob kisses my head and says, "I love you, Katie."

I lie there a moment, trying not to respond, but my body betrays me. Warmth spreads from every place that Jacob's body touches mine—my back, my sides, my hands, my cheek as his rests against mine—and I am filled with a warm glow. It's as if the wall that was built between us the night of the home invasion and discovering the truth about Jacob has dissolved, and it's just Jacob and me. Nothing else matters. I shouldn't respond to his words, but I can't help it. I roll over to face him. "You trimmed your beard," I say, touching his stubble on his cheeks.

"I didn't want you to see me looking like a terrorist." He smiles and shrugs.

"I like it. I can see your dimples." I hold his face in my hands and look him in the eye. My voice shakes when I say, "Tell me again."

He touches my face and caresses my cheek with his thumb. His eyes are liquid brown and tender. "I love you, Katie."

"I believe you," I say.

Jacob kisses me slowly, and it is better than any kiss we'd ever shared before. I tangle my fingers in his hair and pull myself against him. I should put a stop to this. Allowing us to be this close is just going to hurt more tomorrow when he has to disappear again. I can't pull away though. I need this.

I wake slowly. The light from the window penetrates my closed eyelids. It takes a few moments to realize that the presence resting against my back is Stella, not Jacob. Even though I knew he'd have to leave, it doesn't make the disappointment any less devastating. I long to stay in bed, but I know that I have to continue moving forward. I pry my eyes open and see that it's already 7:15. I haven't slept this late nor this well since before...

As I sit up, I notice an envelope on my bedside table. "Katie" is written on the outside in Jacob's handwriting. I open the envelope and pull out a single sheet of paper.

Katie,

As I watch you sleep this morning, you have the sweetest smile on your face, and I am filled with the hope that when you wake, you won't look at last night with regret. I certainly don't. Being with you has given me the courage to face what comes next. I only wish that I could stay with you longer—that I never had to leave you. I hate that you're caught in the middle of my past and me. I want you to know that I'm getting closer to my goal of getting you out of this unharmed. It should be over soon.

I know you have so many questions about my past—about me. I'm not sure you want the answers. There is so much about my life before that I would prefer to protect you from, but I know you have the right to know. If you want to learn more, you know where to look.

I love you!

Jacob

P.S. Please start sleeping in our bed.

What does he mean that he will get me out of this? Doesn't he mean that he will get us out of this? And why does he think I will know where to find the answers about his past? I have no idea where to look. I consider calling him but decide that it's not a good idea. We need to resume our distance from each other, and that includes avoiding phone calls.

Somehow, I make it out the door and to Double Shot at 7:47. I'm running late, but I can still make it to work on time. I get my coffee and turn to leave when someone calls me.

"Katherine."

At first glance, I think it's Jacob, but then my stomach drops. I fight to keep the surprise off of my face. "Juan." I guess I know who's been following me.

"Let's sit for a minute, shall we?" he asks.

I sit in the chair he indicates. My back is to the door, making me feel especially vulnerable. *No matter what he says, don't react.*

Juan puts his elbows on the table and rests his chin on his folded hands. He narrows his eyes as if he's expecting me to speak first. "Well?"

"Well, what?" I ask.

"Aren't you going to thank me for the carnation?"

I lean back and cross my arms across my chest. "You mean the carnation you stole from my mother's grave?"

He raises an eyebrow. "Hmm. You have a point." Straightening, he says, "So, how's my brother doing?"

"I wouldn't know," I say.

Juan smiles, revealing his dimples. Jacob's dimples make him look innocent and trustworthy. Juan's only make him look deceitful. "Oh, come on. You expect me to believe that you haven't seen or heard from Emilio at all?"

"I don't expect that you'll believe anything I say unless it's what you want to hear," I say. I take deep slow breaths.

He laughs. "Oh my. You are so different from my brother's first choice of wives," Juan says. "Gabriela is beautiful but timid. Weak. Perhaps that's why Emilio left. But you, you're feisty. I like you." He sits back in his chair. "It's just too bad that you and my brother aren't really married."

Somehow I'm able to take that blow without flinching.

"Not in the eyes of God anyway. He's still married to Gabriela as far as the Church is concerned. So, I guess you two have been living in sin." Juan winks. "What would Anna think if she could see that her daughter had become an adulteress?"

That one hit hard, and Juan knew it.

My phone rings, and I answer without taking my eyes off Juan. "Katherine Varga."

"Are you okay?" Ed asks.

I look at the clock—8:05. "Sorry, Mr. Howser. I'm running a little late today."

"I assume that you are not okay since you called me Mr. Howser. Where are you?"

"It's too soon to tell, but I'm currently at the Double

Shot. I should be in within the next ten minutes."

"I'm on my way."

"No," I snap. "I'll be there soon." I disconnect the call.

"What do you want, Juan?"

He chuckles. "Just for you to give my brother a message. Tell him it's time."

"Time for what?"

"He'll know."

So many questions swirl in my head. What else has Jacob been keeping from me? "I doubt he'll contact me."

"Oh, I'm pretty sure that he will." Juan stands. "Goodbye, Katherine."

I watch him leave. My legs threaten to give out when I stand. I tell myself to keep moving forward as I hurry across the street. Ed meets me at the door.

"What's going on?" he asks.

"Nothing important," I say and walk past him to the elevator.

I need to speak to Jacob but am not sure how to pull that off. There's no place in this building that's private enough. I decide that, as soon as possible, I'll slip across the street and use the single bathroom at the Double Shot. It needs to be soon because there's no way I'll be able to think about anything else until I've talked to Jacob.

Ed leaves for court at 9:45, and I decide that this time

is as good as any to make my way across the street. I can't help but look around to make sure no one is watching me. I must look incredibly paranoid. I *am* incredibly paranoid.

When I first get to Double Shot, someone is in the restroom. I pace back and forth in front of the door, willing it to open.

"Oh my God," the woman gasps as she opens the door.

"I'm sorry," I say and nearly knock her over as I pass her. I make sure the door is securely locked and retreat to the corner farthest away from it. My hands shake as I dial Jacob's number from my throw-away phone. He answers on the second ring.

"Katie, is everything okay?" His voice is deep and raspy. I must've woken him up.

My voice is barely above a whisper. "I ran into Juan at the Double Shot."

"What?" His tone is urgent.

"I'm fine; don't worry," I say. "He just wanted to talk."

"To talk."

"Well, actually he wanted me to give you a message."

Jacob sighs. "What message?"

"He says that it's time." I try to keep the panic out of my voice. "What does he mean, Jacob?"

Jacob's tone is more controlled when he finally

answers. "I told you that I've been working on a way out for you."

"You mean a way out for us, right?"

"I'm not sure I'll be making it out this time," he whispers.

My voice rises. "What's that supposed to mean? You have to make it out." My heart is racing. "It's them or you, Jacob, and it has to be you. Right?"

"I'm not sure I can survive another round with my brothers."

"You have to. It's them or you. Promise me that it will be you."

"The most important thing is that you get free of this, Katie. That you're safe. And I can promise you that I will do everything in my power to ensure that."

"No," I say. "I won't accept that. How can I help you?"

"I'll not risk you any more than I already have."

"Nonsense," I say. "I will be risking me. It's my choice, Jacob, and I choose to either succeed or not next to you." Jacob doesn't respond. "What next?"

"I'm not sure," he says. "I'll let you know."

"You better."

"Bye, Katie."

"I love you, Jacob."

His voice is husky when he says, "I believe you."

If you want to learn more, you know where to look. Once I begin thinking about it, I know where I'm supposed to look. I stand outside my bedroom door with my hand on the handle. Jacob's right. I can't continue to avoid this room. I take a deep breath and ease the door open.

It does look different. Not only does the new paint and hardwood floors make a difference, but the new arrangement of the furniture gives the room a totally different look. I'd wanted to rearrange the furniture for a couple years, but Jacob had resisted. "The bed should be between those two windows," I'd said. Jacob said that he didn't feel safe sleeping that close to the window. There were now alarms on every window, so I guess he thought it was okay for the bed to be there. I'd been right, it does look better this way.

I look at the closet. The door had been open the night of the home invasion. Victor's body had lain halfway in and halfway out of the door. I almost expect to see a chalk outline where the body used to be, but all I see are shiny dark wood floors. "You're being ridiculous," I tell myself as I swing the door open and enter the closet.

As I slide the dresser aside, I realize that it isn't as heavy as it should be. Pulling open one of the drawers, my heart drops when I see that most of Jacob's clothes are now missing. Of course, he would've come for his clothes while I wasn't here. I'd been so upset with him back then, if I'd been here, I might've shot him.

I finish sliding the dresser aside, revealing the hole in the wall. I need a flashlight. When I return with the flashlight, I notice a switch on the wall just inside the hole. I flip on the light.

It's empty. Not only is it empty, it's been vigorously cleaned. Whatever Jacob had been hiding in here left no evidence. I sit on the floor with my back resting next to the hole. "Where, Jacob?" I say out loud. Resting my head in my hands, racking my brain for another possible hiding place. I run my fingers through my hair and rest my head against the wall. Out of the corner of my eye I see a single key taped to the back of the dresser.

That's it? A key to what? Damn it, Jacob. Holding the

key in one hand and my mother's rosary in the other, I
pace the bedroom. I look under the bed for Jacob's gun
safe. It's not here. I frantically look in every closet top to
bottom for hidden compartments or boxes that might
contain the answers, but whatever I'm looking for, I don't
find it.

Frustrated, I get ready for bed. I climb in the guest
bed and lie there, staring at the ceiling. You know where to
look. Either Jacob has given me more clues than I've
noticed, or he's purposely keeping me from finding the
answers.

How long am I going to continue sleeping in this
room? "I'm not," I say and stomp to the master bedroom.
"Jacob wouldn't like it if I let you sleep in this bed, Stella,
but Jacob isn't here." I pull back the covers on my side of
the bed and find a business card to the bank that's a block
from my work office, and on the back is the number 2097.
The key is to a safety deposit box.

I skip going to the range today. My new Glock is so familiar now that I can probably reduce my range time to once a week. I'm not sure if I can let that part of my daily routine go, even if I don't need the practice. Although I'm better at accepting unexpected events in my day, I still crave the structure and predictability of my routine. Plus, shooting at targets is a great tension releaser.

My hands shake as I remove the items that were in the safety deposit box from my purse. There were two business cards, the first being Agent Stuart's. I already have one, but this one has a handwritten phone number. His personal cell phone perhaps? Why would Jacob have it? Has he been in contact with the agent?

I'm so ready for there to be no more secrets between Jacob and me. The familiar knot forms in my stomach from the betrayal I feel from being so clueless of Jacob's activities, both present and past. The other night, I'd thought I was passed that feeling. I'd accepted that he has secrets that I may never know—secrets that he would need to keep from me for my safety. I'm no longer willing to accept my safety as an excuse to be blocked out of Jacob's life.

The second business card was for Ameris Bank in Jacksonville, Florida, with the number 4630 written on the back. Attached to the card is another safety deposit box key.

The last item I found in the box was a zip drive. I stick it in my laptop and open it. The zip drive contains several folders. The first one is filled with newspaper articles about the Vasquezes. Many of them I've read before, but there were at least twenty that I hadn't seen, some dated before Jacob was born. I skim through the titles and opt to see what's in the other folders.

The second one is more of a diary of every time Jacob interacted with Agent Stuart. Each entry contained a date and a brief summary of what was discussed.

9/15: Overview of cashflow through the bar. Discussed the injuries inflicted by me on JG, HC, and FS.

9/22: Discussed Juan and EJ's roles in Antonio's death.

Think I convinced him that I didn't do it.

Some of the entries are filled with details of what Jacob had disclosed to the agent. Some are just a sentence or two. I start reading one entry dated 10/12 that described the violence Jacob committed on JG, whoever that was. I can't read it all. How could this man be my husband?

The next folder contains arrest records, court documents, and statements that Jacob had given to the police after he, his brothers, and father were arrested. There must be over one hundred pages in this folder. It would take me weeks to read it all.

At the end of the line of folders is a spreadsheet. As I click the icon, a list of names fills the screen. *What did you give me, Jacob?*

I click on Charles Adkins. The page contains Mr. Adkins's personal information—his social security number, address, and phone number. I see that Adkins works for the Water Department in Wheeling, WV. He is married with three children.

After I view the personal information on two more people, I realize what the zip drive contains: the database for Jacob's identity protection website.

I scroll through the names, and one stands out: Anna Lynn Baker. Just before I click on my mother's name, there's a knock at the door, and I nearly knock my chair over when Stella bursts into a barking frenzy. "Stella, hush." I say snapping my fingers. The dog retreats to her bed in the corner of the living room, and a high-pitched whine comes from her instead. I close the laptop and stow the business cards in a hidden compartment of my purse.

Breath, Katherine. My face is hot, and I know that I must look guilty as hell as I open the door. "Agent Stuart."

"Hello, Mrs. Varga." Stuart says smiling. "I'm sorry to bother you at home, but I have a few questions about your husband."

"That makes two of us," I say.

"May I come in?"

"Oh," I say flustered. "Of course, come in." I lead the agent to the couch in the living room. I make a conscience effort to avoid looking at the laptop. "Can I get you something to drink? Lemonade? Iced tea?"

"Tea would be nice. Thank you," he says not sitting on the couch. He's wandering the room as I head to the kitchen. It takes every bit of self-control for me to avoid grabbing my laptop and taking it with me.

Stuart stands in front of the fireplace staring at the photo of Jacob and me that was taken right after our wedding at the courthouse. It's the only photo displayed anywhere in our house. For the first time, I consider just how strange that is.

"You both look happy here," he says gesturing toward the photo.

"We were."

Stuart smiles, probably trying to put me at ease but there is no at ease for me lately. "How long have you been married?"

"Are we married?" I ask, "I mean, Jacob isn't even Jacob."

"Legally? Perhaps not," he says. "I can't speak to that. But, to you and Jacob, you were married, don't you think?"

I stare at the photo above the mantle. "I can't speak for Jacob, but for me, yes, we're married. For almost three years."

The agent makes his way to the couch and sits. Relieved, I sit in an overstuffed chair across from him. "Have you heard from your husband, Mrs. Varga?"

"Call me Katherine," I say realizing that I'm fiddling with my wedding ring. I keep spinning it around and around, thinking that no matter how many times I turn the ring, I'll never find the beginning or the end of it. Marriage is supposed to be like that. I believed our marriage would be forever. But now I don't even know if we're married at all. "I don't know where Jacob is," I say, avoiding the question.

The corner of the agent's mouth rises a little. "That's not what I asked. I asked if you've heard from him."

"Have you?" I ask.

He chuckles humorlessly.

"What will happen to Jacob if you find him?"

He takes a sip of his tea. "When I find him, he'll have to finish his time in prison." As an afterthought, he adds, "and possibly face charges for the murder of the Harty brothers."

"You know he didn't do that," I say. Stuart shrugs. "There's no way for him to avoid prison time?" I ask.

"He disappeared, Katherine. He was supposed to stay in contact in order for his time to be suspended. So, no. There's no way for him to avoid prison this time."

I lean forward in my chair. "What if he had a good reason for breaking contact?"

"Do you know something I don't, Katherine?"

"No." I shake my head. "I don't know why he disappeared on you. It's just that I know my husband, and he wouldn't risk eventual prison time unless he had a good reason."

"Have you had a chance to look over the packet on Emi—Jacob that I gave you?"

I nod.

"Is there anything that stood out to you?"

I lean back in my chair. "Nothing. Everything. It seems like it's all about someone else. I just can't imagine Jacob doing such things."

Stuart rubs his forehead. "Well, I guess neither of us knows your husband as well as we thought."

I can feel the clock on the wall ticking away even though it's actually silent. Maybe it's my heartbeat I'm feeling. It pulses in my ears marking the time of the silence in the room.

"Your husband," Stuart says, "is a good man. He didn't ask to be born into such a—the family that he has. Even though he did terrible things in the past, I don't think that it was in his nature. Deep down, he's good."

I close my eyes, weighing whether to tell the agent that I've seen Jacob. I want to trust this man, but I'm not exactly a reliable judge of trustworthiness. The last thing I want to do is cause Jacob more trouble. "What if he helps you again?"

Stuart does not mask the shock from my words. I'm not sure if it's because he's already in contact with Jacob or if he's surprised that I would hint that I still had influence over my husband. "The deal that he had was not easily secured. And he did run last time. I'm not sure I could pull that off again."

"But it's possible," I say.

"Perhaps."

"Then let's hope one of us finds him before the police or his family does."

Stuart narrows his eyes. "Is he lost, Katherine? Can you contact him?"

"Can you?"

He smiles. "When you next hear from your husband, please tell him to call me."

"If I hear from him, I will try."

Stuart gets up and heads toward the door. He stops and without turning, he says, "We became friends, Emilio and me. I probably shouldn't have allowed that to happen, but you know him." He smiles weakly. "Then he disappeared, and I was sure something terrible happened to him. When I first saw the pictures of the Harty brothers' crime scene, I was relieved that he was okay.

"And then I was furious." Stuart shakes his head. "We were friends, and I trusted him."

I nod. I'd trusted him too.

"You know the longer he's hiding, the harder it will be for me to make a deal."

"I know."

"And the longer he's hiding, the easier it will be for his family to catch up to him. He's in real danger." Turning to look at me, "You're in real danger."

"I know that too." I hold the door for him. "Good night, Agent Stuart."

"Keep in touch," he says, " and stay safe."

I nod and shut the door.

I lock the door behind Stuart and then make my way to every door and window, making sure they're locked too. I make sure all the curtains and blinds are closed before I return to the table.

I open the laptop and stare at my mother's name. I hover the arrow over her name, gathering courage to see what's there. Just seeing her name fills me with emotion. I blink away tears—man, I miss my mother—and click.

I stare at another spread sheet filled with names and personal information. I scroll through the list to see if anything stands out. Then a window pops up.

"Would you like to run the data extraction software?" it reads, with yes and no boxes underneath.

Data extraction? What is Jacob up to? I click on the no button and keep scrolling. Another window pops up. This page contains what looks like complicated computer code. Two words leap from the page: dark web.

Oh my God. I reach for the burner phone.

J acob answers after the second ring. "Is everything okay?"

"You're not selling your clients personal information, are you?"

The silence on the phone is deafening.

"Jacob?"

He sighs noisily. "No—well kind of—but not really."

"What the hell does that mean?"

The words rush out of him rapidly. "We should discuss this in person. Can you meet?"

I run my hands through my tangled hair. "Agent Stuart just left, so I'm not sure I should leave quite yet."

"Stuart?" The panicked tone in my husband's voice makes every nerve in my body shutter. "What did he want?"

I peek out the front window. I shouldn't, but I can't help it. I don't notice anything suspicious outside. "Same thing as always. He wants to know if I've been in contact with you."

Jacob sighs again. "What did you—"

"Don't worry. I lied for you," I say. "I'm getting pretty good at it, even though it goes against my nature." What would the reverend think of me? For that matter, what would my mother think?

"I'm so sorry, Katie. I never wanted you to—"

"Be mixed up in this. I know," I say. "But I am mixed up in it. I even killed someone because of it. We're both in it, and it's time that you stop trying to keep me out."

I wait for Jacob to respond. Ten seconds. Twenty. "And don't tell me that you're trying to protect me because not knowing what's going on is definitely not safe for me. Don't leave me with no way to defend myself."

That did it. "Okay," he murmurs.

"Everything, Jacob," I say firmly. "I need to know it all."

"Meet me at the garage at 10:30," he says. "Pay close attention."

"I know. I'll make sure no one follows me."

Just before I disconnect, Jacob says, "Katie."

"What."

"I love you."

"I know," I say. "I love you too." I shouldn't; I don't want to, but love is irrational.

Wanting to give myself plenty of time to make sure I'm not being followed, I leave my house at 9:30. I drive in the opposite direction of the parking garage, not sure where I'm heading. If I don't know, then whoever might be following me won't know either.

How did I get here? How did my life become this? I'd had a normal childhood. I followed the rules. I never lied or cheated. I was loyal and patient and went out of my way to be kind to everyone. I was a preacher's kid for Christ's sake. When Melanie and I sat in her bedroom dreaming about being teachers one day, I'd never have imagined that instead I would become a legal secretary, the daughter of a murderer, the wife of a man who isn't whom he'd said he was, the killer of an invader, and a person who has to look in her rearview mirror almost as much as she looks out the windshield in front of her to make sure that some killer or law enforcement officer isn't waiting to sneak up on her to catch her with her fugitive, probably not legal, husband.

Preacher's kid, indeed.

I turn from the wrong lane without using my blinker

on numerous occasions, so if I have a follower, he or she will have to do the same or risk losing me. By the time I reach the garage, not one other car is anywhere near me. I'm ten minutes early, but Jacob is waiting for me when I arrive.

As Jacob climbs in, the interior light reveals his deep dimpled smile. "God, you look good," he says, shutting the door and leaving us in darkness.

He looks good too, really good, but I don't say it. Instead, I say, "Spill."

"What, no warmup conversation?" He tries for humor, but the tremor in his voice reveals what he's trying to hide behind the dimples.

It's difficult, but I keep silent. I wonder if he knows how much my insides are squirming at his discomfort. Part of me wants to tell him that it's okay if he still needs time before he reveals his plan. The other more insistent part screams that he's had more than enough time.

"Okay," he says. "Where should I start?"

"Tell me about the names on the zip drive and what they have to do with the dark web."

Jacob's hands are pressed together, bumping against his nose while he thinks. Then he drops his hands and says, "The names on the list aren't real. I mean, they're kind of real, but not really. It's real enough, hopefully, to fool my brothers."

"Stop talking in circles, Jacob."

"I'm sorry. The plan to sell identities to the dark web began years ago, when I was informing on my family to Stuart." Jacob leans back, resting his head on the headrest and stares out the windshield into the blackness. "It had been almost eight months of me lying to my family and revealing enough family secrets to Stuart to get them put away. I was getting restless and afraid of being found out. I started to consider changing my name and getting the hell out of there before my father found out and had me killed.

"One day, I was researching how to obtain a new identity on the dark web when my brothers caught me. I had to think fast. I made up this plan about how I was going to start an identity protection business and after I grew the business sufficiently, I was going to sell all the information and make a ton of money. I meant it to be this wild, impossible but believable idea. I thought they'd razz me about it and have a good laugh. But they didn't. They wanted in."

Jacob runs his fingers through his hair. "As I talked about how I could program the whole protection site with a back door that I could all at once extract all the information and sell it to the highest bidder, I realized that it wouldn't be impossible. My brothers were so excited, they asked me how soon I could have the program ready."

"So, is that what you were doing this whole time? Setting your clients up to have their identities stolen?"

Jacob shakes his head. "No, Katie. I promise. All my research on how the dark web works made my clients safer."

"Then why, Jacob?"

His dark eyes lock on mine. "When my brothers found out about my company, they thought—"

"They thought you were doing it without them," I say.

"When I told them that I wasn't going to betray my clients, they didn't believe me."

"Wait," I say. "You've talked to Juan and EJ?"

"Not in person, but through other means."

I squeeze my eyes shut. "What other means?"

Jacob lays everything out for me. At least, I think it's everything. I can't understand all of the technical stuff, but he is patient as he explains how he's using a mixture of real and false identity information to build a new site that will fool his brothers.

"But, when they find out, they'll kill you," I say.

"No. If they find out, they'll go after you. That would be worse."

"You're going to work with Agent Stuart again, aren't you?"

"That's my hope."

"Have you spoken to him?" I ask.

"Not directly."

So that's why the agent came to see me. He has to know that I've been lying to him.

"That reminds me," Jacob says. "Give me your

burner."

My stomach drops, and I think that my husband's leaving me with no way to get in touch with him. He pulls another burner out of his pocket. "Use this one instead. That one needs to be destroyed."

Relief overwhelms me. "What can I do, Jacob?"

"Nothing," he says, but before I could object, he adds, "Nothing yet, but soon."

I almost whine when I say, "How long?"

"Soon," he says simply. And I want to punch him in the face.

After a few evenings combing through the folders on Jacob's zip drive, I decide that I've learned enough about my husband's previous life. No matter what he's done, and he's done plenty of bad things, I'm sure he's not that guy anymore. He's still dangerous, but only when he has to be, and I can live with that.

I keep my daily routine, only I go to the range every other day instead of daily. And I wait. I wait for Jacob to give me instructions. When I'm at home, I do a lot of pacing. I hate waiting. I'm ready for this all to be over.

The first day that I don't get a text from Jacob is

concerning. The second day, I'm officially worried. By the third day, I'm convinced that something terrible has happened to my husband. My emotions swing from fury to terror. I break my routine and leave work early—I can't concentrate anyway—and head straight home.

As I swing the door to my house open, it's silent. Eerily silent. I know that I set the alarm when I left this morning. Stella greets me at the door whining with her belly low to the ground. I pat her on the head and close the door quietly. Turning carefully, I slip my gun from my belly holster. Stella trots out of the entryway. I creep through the entryway to my living room and stop dead.

Jacob is lying on the floor beaten and bloody. Stella lies next to him as if she's guarding him. She whines when she sees me, but she doesn't leave Jacob's side. He looks dead.

Legs weak and trembling, I kneel beside Jacob and gently touch his cheek. It's warm; thank God. "Jacob."

One of his eyes flutters open, and he smiles. He smiles! Although it's not a real deep-dimple Jacob smile because his face is so swollen. His left eye only opens a crack. "Katie," he rasps, "you should see the other guy."

"Who did this to you?" I ask blinking tears away.

He licks his lips. "Not sure."

"Why are you on the floor?"

He closes his eyes. "Didn't want to get blood on the couch."

"Don't be stupid, Jacob. Let me help you up."

He winces as he moves slightly. "Can you get me some water first?"

When I return with Jacob's water, he is sitting hunched over with his forehead resting on his knees. He inhales sharply as he straightens up enough to drink. He's so weak that I have to help him hold the glass.

"See if you can get to your knees," I say holding his arm firmly to keep him from toppling over. He stays on his knees for several seconds before lifting his right one to place his foot on the floor. "Take your time."

Jacob leans heavily on me as he stands. He gasps, his breathing rapid and shaky. "I shouldn't be here," he says.

"Nonsense," I say. "Now that you're up, do you want to try to make it to our bedroom?"

"I can't stay here, Katie. It's not safe."

"You're staying here, Jacob." He takes a deep breath to speak again, but I stop him. "I mean it, Jacob. You're in no condition to leave here unless it's in an ambulance."

"No doctors," he mumbled.

"No doctors," I say, "unless I don't have a choice."

Jacob trembles and increases the pressure of his weight on me. He's probably too weak to make it all the way to the bedroom. We shuffle slowly to the couch where I help lower him to a seated position. He leans his head on the back of the couch and closes his eyes, his forehead tight with pain.

"Where does it hurt?"

He opens his, not good, but less injured eye and looks at me. "Be easier to tell you what doesn't."

I manage a slight smile. "Where doesn't it hurt?"

He closes his eye. "Don't know."

Leaning forward, I rest my head in my hands with my elbows on my knees. A few tears escape. He could've been killed. Why didn't they kill him? The reason doesn't matter. I'm just glad that he's alive. By the look of his face, his injuries are extensive. I need to take a closer look. Where do I start?

Jacob manages to reach out and touch my lower back. "I'll be fine, Katie. It's just a scratch."

I chuckle. "This isn't funny, Jacob. You could've died—you still might." Tears drip down my face onto my legs. Tears of relief. Sympathetic tears for Jacob's pain. Tears of fear and frustration that this whole thing still isn't over. I don't even attempt to wipe them away.

"You really don't know who did this?"

"They put something over my head before I could get a look, but I know it was instigated by my family."

"If that were the case," I say, "why cover your head?"

Jacob shrugs, then winces. "Probably so I wouldn't fight back." The corner of his mouth lifts. "I did get a few good hits in there though."

I shake my head.

"EJ wasn't there, I know that."

"How do you know?"

His good eye grabs mine. "Because he wouldn't have stopped until I was dead. This was done by people who wanted me to live. At this point, they need me alive."

"They need you to get the identities."

He nods.

"Do you think you can make it to the bedroom now?"

Jacob raises his eyebrows and winces. "I'm a mess, Katie. You don't want this in your bed."

His shirt and jeans are covered in blood. For the first time I notice that his knuckles are bruised and bloody. He did get a few good licks in. "Come on," I say. "I think I still have clean sweatpants and a t-shirt for you to wear." I know that I do; I've been wearing them to bed almost every night.

Jacob's legs are a little steadier as we walk to the bedroom, and by the time we get there, Jacob thinks he can manage a shower.

"Leave the door unlocked, so I can get in if you need me."

He smiles weakly. "I'll be sure to need you then," he says, and I chuckle. "Seriously though." He inhales sharply, winces, and sighs. "I could use help taking off my shirt." He raises his arms slightly to show how painful it is for him.

"Sit," I say, and he sits on the edge of the bed. I slide my hand under his shirt to ease his arm out without him having to raise it. Jacob sucks in a breath between his teeth. "I'm sorry."

When I finally manage to free Jacob from his shirt, I'm horrified at the sight of him. His whole left side is covered in a dark purple bruise. I follow the bruise to his back which is just as covered.

"My God, Jacob."

Jacob grabs my hands, forcing me to look into his face. "I'm fine, Katie. It's nothing that I haven't been through before."

"You've been beaten like this before?"

He nods. "And I'm ashamed to admit that I've given my share too."

Jacob stands and pulls me into his arms, and I don't even try to stop the tears. This man, who so gently comforts me, who protects me, who makes me laugh, who loves me, is the same man who could inflict the same depth of harm that has been done to him. How do I reconcile those things? "I'm scared, Jacob."

"I know. I'm scared too, but we'll get through this, even if it kills me."

I lift my head, so I can see his face. "You are not allowed to die, Jacob. Do you hear me?"

He smiles. "I'll try not to disappoint you."

"I love you."

Jacob cradles my face in his hands. "I love you, Katie—more than you can possibly know."

29

I sleep like a baby, waking at least every hour, staring at Jacob until my eyes can't manage to stay open, and then drifting off. Jacob sleeps like the dead. I only know that he's not by the moaning that comes from him when he moves in his sleep.

The darkness behind the curtain gives way to daylight as I stare at my husband. I can't believe he's here in our bed. I've missed him immensely. I've dreamed of waking with him next to me every night since the incident, but I never imagined that the only way I could get him to stay was for him to be too injured to leave. Even now, I'm afraid that he'll leave as soon as he's awake. He shouldn't be alone right now—he's in no shape to be alone—but I'm sure that as soon as I leave for work, he'll force himself to leave. He'll say that it's for my safety, but I'm more worried about his well-being than my own at the moment.

I creep into the bathroom to make a phone call, so I don't disturb Jacob. I call the office and leave a voicemail with the receptionist, explaining that I won't make it to work today. "I probably won't be there tomorrow or Friday either. Believe me, nobody there wants what I have," I say, hoping that I've put enough misery in my tone to be convincing.

I open the door and jump when I hear Jacob's voice. "What have I done to you?" He smiles, shaking his head. "Missing work. Lying about being sick. Not acceptable behavior from a preacher's daughter."

I laugh. "You're forgetting who the preacher was that raised me. You know, the one who cheated on my mom, killed her, and then lied about it." I never thought I'd be able to speak so lightly about the worst thing that ever happened to me. Until now. What happened then was a split-second decision by a man who felt backed into a corner—a decision that he regretted for the rest of his life. Everything now isn't happening from a split-second decision, but calculated choices by first Jacob's family and now Jacob. It's more like a life-or-death chess match or a staring contest, each side waiting for the other to blink.

Jacob's brothers must be getting terribly restless, having taken such measures to force his next move. Or it could be that they just wanted to get revenge for Jacob's part in sending them and their father to prison. What scares me the most at the moment is that I'm sure their revenge is not complete.

Jacob sleeps the better part of two days. When he wakes, he forces himself to shuffle around the house, wincing and groaning. He refused anything stronger than Tylenol for the pain. I even offered to go to the liquor store and buy whiskey or beer, which I find repulsive, but he refused.

Ed texts me on Thursday:

(Ed) Are you really sick or does this have to do with Jacob?

(Me) Is this my lawyer speaking or my boss?

(Ed) Are you safe?

(Me) I have a top-of-the-line security system and firearms scattered throughout my house.

(Me) I'm quite safe.

(Ed) That's not what I mean.

(Me) I know.

(Ed) Be careful.

(Me) I'm always careful

(Ed) Call if you need me

(Me) I will. And if I'm not back on Monday morning, feel free to replace me. :)

(Ed) You're irreplaceable.

(Me) See you Monday.

Friday morning, Jacob enters the kitchen and says, "Well, no more blood in my urine, so my kidneys must be better."

"You had blood in your urine? Why didn't you tell me?"

He smiles wide. The swelling in his face has gone down significantly, so his dimples shine brightly. "Because I didn't want to see that look on your face or for you to panic and take me to the hospital."

"You could have serious internal injuries, Jacob."

He puts his hands on my shoulders. "I told you, I've been through this before. I knew it was nothing to worry about." He kisses me on the cheek and says, "What smells so good?"

We sit at the table to eat breakfast, but all I can manage is to move the scrambled eggs around on my plate. I can't believe Jacob didn't tell me about the blood in his urine. I don't know if it's that I'm just angry or if it's that I feel lied to. Again. I sit in silence, not trusting myself to speak.

"I've been thinking," Jacob says. "You now know everything about my nefarious past, but I know very little about yours."

I smile slightly. "I was a perfect, obedient, truthful child who followed all the rules to the letter."

"Seriously," he says, laughing. "It's only fair that I

know something that you did against your parents' wishes."

I put my fist in front of my mouth and look to the side. "Well, there was this one time." Jacob leaned forward and placed his forearms on the table. "Melanie was spending the night with me one Friday. Melanie was my best friend growing up. We always talked about being teachers together and having adjoining classrooms at Harrison Elementary.

"Anyway, Melanie was more adventurous than me, and we were bored, so she convinced me to sneak out of the house after my parents went to bed. I was terrified that my parents would hear the front door opening, so… You know the doors that led to the cellar at the beginning of The Wizard of Oz?" Jacob nodded. "Well, we had a set of those that led to our basement. We snuck out those instead, which was ridiculous because they were way louder than the front door.

"We somehow managed to escape unnoticed and went to a party Eddie Newman was having in some hayfield at his farm."

Jacob beams. "And?"

"And I had a terrible time. There was beer, which would have been enough to entice me to leave. I mean, what if the cops showed up and the reverend found out? Most of my friends that were there were well beyond tipsy and loud and—let's say extremely flirty. People were making out all over the place. I think I lasted all of fifteen minutes before I begged Mel to go home with me."

"Did the reverend find out?"

"No, thank God," I say. "I still can't think about that night without feeling sick to my stomach from guilt."

Jacob roars with laughter and then winces. "That's it? That's the worst thing you did growing up? How old were you?"

"Sixteen, seventeen." I shrug.

Jacob's smile disappears and his face loses its color. "What must you think about me and all I've done?"

"None of that," I say. "Your turn."

"You know everything," he says softly.

"No. I don't." I lean forward smiling. "I want to know something good about your childhood. With Antonio maybe?"

"Antonio and I had some good times, most of them involved all kinds of reprehensible acts." He grins. "There were a couple years when I was in grade school—third and fourth grades. I had this friend who used to invite me over to his house all the time. He had a normal family. You know, he had a dad that wasn't a criminal and a stay-at-home mom who always had homemade cookies waiting for us when we got home from school. He had an older brother who he looked up to and a sister who he teased relentlessly. That was when I first realized how not normal my family really was.

"His dad had built a treehouse in the backyard that we hung a Girls not allowed sign on, which made his sister cry, so we had to take it down." He chuckles. "I ate dinner at their house two or three times a week. At the end of our fourth-grade year, Jacob announced that his dad got transferred to West Virginia and that they were moving as soon as school was out." He shakes his head. "Needless to say, I was devastated."

"That's why you changed your name to Jacob."

He nods. "It's also the reason I came to West Virginia when I ran from North Carolina."

"Do you know where Jacob is now?"

He shakes his head. "No. I've thought about finding him so many times, but I didn't want him to know how I turned out."

"I think you've turned out pretty well."

"Well, I took a hell of a road to get here, and I still can't seem to get away from my past."

"You will, Jacob. I believe in you."

He smiles. "And it's that belief that gives me hope that I can get you out of this unharmed."

"You mean both of us—get us both out unharmed." I hold my palm out on the table, offering him to take it. Jacob stares at the table rubbing his forehead with one hand and putting his other on top of mine. "Jacob, look at me."

He rests his forehead on his hand and lifts his eyes to mine.

"You're getting us both out."

His expression is pained. "Katie, I'm not—"

"Don't, Jacob," I say. "Don't tell me that you're not sure you'll make it out alive this time. You have to, damn it. Promise me."

He takes a deep breath to answer when the doorbell rings three times in quick succession.

We share a look, and Jacob heads to the bedroom and shuts the door behind him. I gather the dishes, open the dishwasher, and place the whole stack on top of the bottom rack.

I hurry to the door. Breathe Katherine. I pull open the door.

"Have you heard from him?" Agent Stuart says pushing past me into the house.

"Is something wrong?"

Stuart swings around to face me. He steps forward, pressing on my personal space. "I lost contact. Be honest with me now, Katherine. Have you spoken to your husband in the last week?"

"Wait," I say, stalling. "You've been in contact with Jacob?" He leans forward and I force myself to stand firm.

"No more avoiding the question. Answer me, Katherine."

I hadn't realized that the man could be so intimidating. His usual demeanor is calm and nonthreatening, which makes his current behavior more unsettling.

"It's okay, Katie," Jacob says from the hallway.

My stomach, which had been in my throat since answering the door, plummets. I place my hand in front of my mouth and close my eyes.

"I should arrest you right now, you son of a bitch." Stuart says, and then pointing at me, "You too."

"Leave her out of it," Jacob says calmly and turns toward the living room. The agent and I follow him. Jacob is sitting on the couch looking as if this was just a normal day with nothing much going on. "You want something? Coffee? Tea?"

Stuart sighs and runs his hand over his head. "Coffee would be nice."

I don't move, not because I don't want to retrieve the coffee, but because the shock of having the agent who's been trying to capture my husband in the same room with him.

"You could arrest me, buddy, or I could help you get my brothers."

Stuart lets out a loud sigh. "What do you got?" he says and sits on the chair across from Jacob.

That unlocks my legs, and I go to the kitchen.

Jacob runs down a list of Juan and EJ's criminal activities that he's been gathering evidence on. It's a long list. If he and the agent can manage it, they'll go away for much longer than they did the last time.

Stuart listens without interrupting. He nods and rubs his beard and bites his lip until Jacob's words run out. "Plan?" the agent says.

Jacob gives more details in this telling of the plan than he did when he was telling me—probably because Stuart understands it better. Jacob explains how he's creating false identities that he will convince his brothers that he will sell on the dark web. Stuart asks several questions that Jacob answers without hesitating. He's obviously thought a lot about this over the past few months. Stuart makes suggestions, which Jacob considers and improves upon. As I listen, I see how well these two work together, and their mutual regard is obvious.

"What about me?" I ask.

Jacob wrinkles his forehead, confused by my question. "What do you mean?"

"How do I fit in the plan?"

"You're not getting anywhere near this," he says.

I can feel my face heat up. "Oh no, Jacob. I'm not sitting here waiting while you get yourself killed. I'm going with you no matter what you say, so you might as well give me a job."

"No."

My shoulders tense up, and my nails dig into my palms from clenching my fists. "I'm coming."

"No," he says. His dark eyes bore into mine. Another time, I might find his look frightening. Now it just angers me.

My words seep out through gritted teeth. "You're not leaving me out of this."

"Wait, Jacob," Stuart says. "This could be good." Jacob shifts his glare to the agent. "She could be a needed distraction."

"A distraction for me," Jacob says. "I can't risk her,

and that's final."

"Think about it," Stuart says. "They'd think by having both of you, they can use her against you. When in fact, she's helping you."

"How?"

Stuart stands and starts pacing the room. "You, my friend, are the best at using your assets. That woman right there is your absolute best one. Figure it out."

Jacob says nothing, which I interpret as a good sign.

"I'm not some helpless damsel in distress," I say. "I can take care of myself, and they don't know that."

When Jacob answers, his voice is calmer. "I don't like it. I can't risk you."

"You're not risking me; I'm risking myself."

Jacob closes his eyes tight and shakes his head. "Let me think about it."

"How much time do you need?" Stuart says.

"Week, maybe ten days." Jacob says. "You?"

Agent Stuart nods. "I can probably get my part arranged by then. How do I get ahold of you?"

"Give him your burner, Katie."

"The number or the phone?"

Jacob smiles slightly. "The phone." The look on my face betrays the panic I feel from parting with my one means of communicating with my husband when he's not here. "It's okay. Trust me."

Trust. Such a simple word but a terribly difficult thing to do. I used to be a very trusting person. I thought that most people were inherently good and trustworthy. I only lost trust when someone deserved it. The problem is that the first person to ever lose my trust was the reverend. He'd not only broken my trust for him, but also my ability to trust. There are no words powerful enough that he could say, no deed good enough to make me trust him again. At least that's what I told myself. And, now he's gone, and I will never know for sure if I am capable of healing.

And then came Jacob. I trusted him with my whole heart. And he'd broken that trust too. Broken me. But, for some reason, I want nothing more than to trust him again. Why is that? Is love really that blind? Or am I just so afraid of having to start my life over again that I'll do anything not to lose what's left of the one I have?

Can I trust Jacob? That's the question that floats around in my head the whole weekend that Jacob and I are together. There are some moments when we almost forget about the danger we'd be facing and are able to be ourselves. For the first time since the incident, I'm able to laugh. I relax with Jacob and feel safe, despite the fact that neither one of us is safe. I'm not sure whether I'll ever truly be safe again.

I kiss Jacob goodbye on Monday morning, knowing that he won't be here when I return. Driving to work, I can't shake the fear gripping me. Fear for Jacob. Fear that I'll never see him again. Fear that he'll try to implement his plan without me. Fear that he'll betray my trust again. And, perhaps the greatest fear, fear of living the rest of my life without him.

I smile at Becky, the receptionist, as I pass by the front desk, hoping my smile looks genuine. It probably does; I'm getting so much better at lying. Becky hands me a stack of pink message slips, and I thank her as gracefully as I can manage.

I look through the window of Ed's office, and he waves me in. Sighing, I set my Double Shot coffee down and stuff my purse into a desk drawer. I take a couple steps and then return to pick up my coffee. It's best if I have reinforcements.

"It's good to see that you're feeling better," Ed says, crossing his arms across his chest and standing behind his desk.

I sit in the chair in front of his desk and try my best to look relaxed. I swallow hard in a desperate attempt to keep my breakfast from making a reappearance. "Am I in trouble?"

Ed chuckles and sits in his chair. "What's going on, Katherine?" I hesitate to answer, praying that I don't say the wrong thing. "Katherine?"

"Are you my lawyer right now or my boss?"

"Do you need a lawyer?"

Do I? I have been aiding and abetting a wanted fugitive. Does it make a difference that Agent Stuart knows this? Would it make a difference to Ed? I'm pretty sure he would support me even if he disagreed with me. But he's still my boss, and I don't want to lose my job. I smile and shake my head. "Aren't we a pair."

Ed leans forward and puts his forearms on the desk. "You can trust me."

Trust. That word. He has no idea how much emotional garbage that word carries for me.

But Ed has never given me any reason not to trust him. He was there for me that awful night. He sat beside me as I learned horrible truths about my husband. He didn't judge me then. He didn't doubt me when I said that I knew nothing about Jacob's past. He's the only person in my life who has any idea who my husband had been. I just wonder if it's possible for him to see Jacob for who he is now, whoever that is.

No. I know Jacob. I know that he loves me and that he wants to protect me. He is gentle and kind and loving. And dangerous.

"How about we talk as friends," Ed says, "and if at any time this discussion seems to be going in the direction of your needing an attorney, we'll switch it up."

He doesn't mention whether my job was in jeopardy, and I choose not to bring it up. I tell him everything, well almost everything. I leave out the actual plan mostly because I don't know most of it. Ed just knows that there is one. I also don't tell him that I've been in contact with Jacob for weeks; although, I think he suspects it.

"What's your part in this plan?" Ed asks, brows furrowed.

I bite my lip. "It's probably best if you don't know."

"I think," Ed says, "It's best if you let Jacob handle his dangerous family and stay out of it."

"Not an option."

"Why?" he asks, angry this time. "Why does he need you? Why is he putting you in danger? Again."

I lean forward and put my hand on the edge of Ed's desk. "He's not. I'm putting myself in danger."

"Why?" Ed's voice gets louder.

So does mine. "Because he's my husband. Because I'm terrified that something is going to happen to him. I have to be there. I can't sit at home and worry and wonder what's going on."

"How is your being there going to keep him safe?"

My vision blurs from unshed tears, and I blink them away. "He'll be more careful because he'll think he needs to protect me."

"Doesn't he?"

"I can protect myself," I say and almost believe it.

Ed takes a noisy breath in and lets it out in a rush. "There's nothing I can say to get you to change your mind?"

I shake my head.

Slumping in his chair, Ed says, "What happened to that sweet, innocent, timid girl I hired?"

I smile weakly. "She killed someone and realized that her black and white predictable world never really existed." We stare at each other without speaking. Ed nods. "I can't keep letting life just happen to me," I say. "I have to take control—to take responsibility for what I can control."

"I'm terrified for you."

"I know."

"I can't imagine losing you," Ed says gently. "You scared?"

I shrug and chuckle. "Maybe, a little."

As expected, Jacob is gone when I get home from work. Resting on my pillow is a replacement burner phone. There's a text message waiting when I power it on.

(Jacob) You okay?

(Me) Yes. You?

It takes a few minutes for his response to appear. I bring the phone with me to the closet to get changed.

(Jacob) I am now.

(Jacob) I love you

(Me) I love you more.

(Jacob) Impossible

I smile, realizing that I do indeed trust this man, even though I probably shouldn't. I can't wait for this all to be over so life can be normal again. What the hell is normal anyway?

31

I jerk awake. Someone is in my house. I roll off the bed and crouch low, keeping the bed between me and the door. Why isn't Stella barking? Reaching under the bed for my bedside gun safe, I find nothing. I lie on my stomach and look, but it's too dark to see. I rip my cell phone from its charger and turn on the flashlight.

There's nothing under the bed. My heart is pounding, and I'm having a difficult time catching my breath. I remember putting my gun in the safe just before I climbed into bed a few hours ago. Both of my guns were there. I'm sure of it. Stella was also with me, but where is she now?

Gun. I need a gun. Think, Katherine, think. The cubby in the closet. I run to the closet and pull the door open and trip over Victor's dead body.

My scream wakes me for real this time, and Stella flies off the bed. I'm sitting, sweating, and sobbing, when I realize what's really woken me is the ringing of my burner phone. I take a long breath in and let it out slowly before answering.

"Are you awake this time, Katie?"

My heart is still pounding. "What?" My head is foggy—my thoughts slow. I blink my eyes a few times.

"Katie?"

"Hmm?"

"You okay?"

I walk over to the closet and pull the door open. No Victor. "Just having a hard time waking up. I was in the middle of a very realistic dream."

"Good dream?"

"Not really." I'm on my hands and knees, pulling out my gun safe. Both guns are there. "Victor's body was in the closet again."

"I'm so sorry, Katie," Jacob murmurs.

"Stop apologizing," I say, annoyed. "I'm awake now."

"Can you be ready to leave in thirty minutes?"

It's time. What had taken what seemed like forever to get here seems too soon now. "I'll be ready in twenty."

"I'll pick you up."

I set my alarm for the next morning so that I remember to call Rebecca and have her take Stella to the kennel. I'll have to leave a key for her somewhere and leave the alarm off. My stomach clenches at the thought of leaving my house unprotected, but Jacob and I won't be here anyway.

Jacob's driving a small black SUV. I don't ask where he got it, I just climb in. It's probably best if I don't ask questions that I'm not sure I want the answer to.

Instead of heading out of town, we pull up in front of a small Catholic church. "I need to make a confession before we go," he says, smiling weakly. "Just in case."

"The church will be open at 3:23 in the morning?"

Jacob smiles. "The priest is a friend of mine." He makes a call on his phone and says, "We're here."

When we first step inside, the church is dimly lit. The only lights are a red lamp next to a golden box and a spotlight shining on the crucifix behind the altar.

The suffering Jesus.

"This is Father Michael," Jacob says.

"Katherine," Father Michael says. "It's wonderful to finally meet you."

I smile and nod. I should make eye contact with the man, but I can't seem to take my eyes away from the sheer beauty of the place. I'd never seen the inside of a Catholic church before—the reverend would've cringed at the very thought of entering such a place.

Maybe it's because it's the middle of the night, and we're the only ones here. Maybe it's the spotlight shining on the body of Jesus. Maybe it's the silence, but something about the place felt...holy. I didn't want to break the spell with awkward small talk.

I can see Father Michael's smile out of the corner of my eye as he watches me take in the room—not room— this is more than that. Not just a building; it was a sanctuary.

"Let me get more light," the priest says, and I notice his faint accent. Father Michael is much shorter than Jacob, maybe about my height, with dark brown hair and eyes. He's dressed in black slacks and dress shirt. His priest's collar hangs with one side loose, which speaks of his familiarity with Jacob.

As Father Michael disappeared through a door to the side of the alter, I started slowly making my way down the center aisle toward the lighted crucifix. Jacob drops to one knee makes the sign of the cross just in front of the altar. I narrow my eyes at his gesture.

"Catholic thing," he says, smiling.

I approach the statue of Mary holding infant Jesus who, ironically, is holding a small cross in his tiny fist. Pictures line both sides of the church. The lights turn on, and I make my way to the first one. Jesus stands in front of a several men. Under the picture reads, "Jesus is condemned to die."

I move to the second. Jesus is hunched below the weight of the cross, a crown of thorns on his head. The words say, "Jesus carries his cross."

"The Stations of the Cross," Father Michael says. I hadn't realized that he'd came up behind me. "They tell a story—a story about the day Jesus died. Every Friday during Lent, we take time as a community to remember and pray."

I nod. We pass "Jesus falls for the first time" and "Jesus meets his mother." It's the first time I considered the possibility of Jesus's own mother watching her son's agony. We move on past the one where Simon helps Jesus carry his cross. The sixth one stops me short.

For some reason, this one fills me with emotion. "Wow," I whisper.

"Veronica wipes the face of Jesus," Father Michael says. "This one always gets me too."

Father Michael steps back, allowing me to step closer to the picture. "All those people watched Jesus beaten so severely that he could barely stand. And then he was forced to carry the cross upon which he would die," he said. "No one spoke up. No one tried to stop it. And yet, Veronica fearlessly emerged from the crowd to offer tenderness.

"She had to know that she put herself in great danger by showing kindness to the condemned. She acted anyway—because he was her Jesus."

Father Michael speaks Spanish to Jacob, and for some reason the fluency in which Jacob answers surprises me, which is ridiculous after having met his mother. Her accent was pronounced, yet I never noticed Jacob having one.

Placing his hand on the small of my back and leaning up next to my ear, Jacob says. "I'm going to his office. Be back in a few."

Nodding, I look at Veronica, awed by her courage. Shamed by my cowardice. After all, I was the one who ran from my home and family because I didn't want to face the tragedy that happened there.

I ran, never planning to look back. I would've run away from Jesus. Away from the crowd. Away from the streets. Away.

You're not running now. The voice wouldn't have been audible had anyone else been present, yet I heard it loud and clear.

I peruse past the rest of the pictures, pausing at the one where Jesus's body is taken down from the cross and laid in his mother's lap.

The men return quietly. Jacob slides into the front pew and kneels down.

"Come, Katherine," Father Michael says. "Let's talk while he says his prayers of penance." My feet seem stuck to the floor. "Do not worry," he says, grinning widely. "No confession. Just talk."

Fr. Michael's office was small but tidy. His desk was cleared of everything except a desktop computer and a small crucifix. Taped to the top of the desk facing so that his visitor could read it is a paper that says "Act of

Contrition" across the top. "Jacob tells me that this is your first time in a Catholic church."

I smile as I sit in the chair in front of his desk. "The reverend would've never allowed it."

"Your father?" I nod. "Is it so different than the church you grew up in.?"

I chuckle. "A bit," I say. "In the words of the reverend, 'We focus on the resurrection, not the death.'"

Father Michael grins and sits up straight as if he is preparing himself for a debate. "But without the death, the resurrection means nothing."

I raise my eyebrows. "He said something close to that the last time I saw him. He told me that until he contemplated on the suffering Christ, he couldn't embrace his victory." I finally understand my father's words.

"Wise man."

I shrug.

Father Michael leans forward, places his elbows on his desk, and rests his chin on his clasped hands. "Have you forgiven him for killing your mother?"

That gets my attention. "A few times," I say. "I'll probably have to forgive him several more times before it sticks."

"Wise woman, like your father."

Looking toward the bookshelf, I say, "It's hard for me to see the wisdom of the man who murdered my mother."

Father Michael says nothing as if he's allowing my words to marinate before responding.

I close my eyes and see Victor lying on my closet floor. "I guess the reverend and I are more alike than I would like." Feeling his gaze on me, I can't bear to look at him.

"You know how I knew you hadn't forgiven him before you told me?" I turn toward him. "You said the reverend wouldn't allow you to enter a Catholic church, not your father wouldn't."

Choosing my words carefully and narrowing my eyes, I say, "He stopped being my father when he choked the life out of my mother."

"Did he?"

Angry tears betray me as they slide down my face. No matter how many times I deny the reverend…my father, it doesn't change the fact that I'm his daughter. I don't want to be the daughter of a murderer. I never dreamed that I'd become a killer too.

Father Michael grabs a box of tissues from the shelf behind him and slides them across the desk to me. "Your father murdered your mother; you killed an intruder. That's very different, Katherine."

Grabbing a tissue and wiping my eyes, I bite my lip. "He took my mother; I took a father away from his children."

"He would've killed you."

"You can't know that. I didn't even hesitate. I just pulled the trigger. Jacob said to take care of him, and I did." I cover my face—my shame.

"Katherine," he says gently. "Armed men broke into your house, attacked your husband, and killed your dog. Do you really think the man would have left you unharmed? And if he did, which, by the way, I doubt very much, do you think he would've spared Jacob?"

I'd never considered that.

"I believe you not only saved yourself but you saved your husband as well."

Holding Father Michael's gaze, I take a deep breath and let it out slowly. Smiling weakly, I say, "I thought this wasn't going to be a confession."

He laughs.

"Jacob thinks he's going to die," I say.

"And what do you think?"

I feel my jaw tightening. "Not if I can help it." Shaking my head, "I never dreamed that I'd be faced with the choice to kill or be killed. For sure, I never imagined that I'd be able to shoot someone, yet here I am, willingly charging into a situation where I might have to do it again."

A small crease forms in the middle of Father Michael's forehead. "Are you afraid you'll have to kill again?"

I've already resigned myself to the fact that I may have to kill again. I've practiced shooting until I can hit a target center mass almost in my sleep. Two guns are strapped to my body, one across my belly and one on my ankle. I don't want to have to take another life, but I will. To save Jacob, I most definitely will.

"No," I say. "I'm afraid it will be easier the next time."

We get as far as Savannah before we stop at a hotel. Jacob is exhausted, but I'd slept on and off all day, so I couldn't settle. I move to the chair and watch Jacob sleep. *Please, God. Don't let this be the last time I get to watch him sleep.* Every time I try to imagine my life without Jacob, I can't bear it. I just keep going over different scenarios in my head, trying to plan how I'll keep my husband alive. But I know that I can't possibly think of everything.

Jacob rolls over and reaches out toward my side of the bed. "I'm here," I whisper, and climb into bed. He pulls me against his chest and kisses my hair, and I melt into him. Please, God.

"Do you think they'll take us to the cabin?" I say, my stomach knotted with fear.

"No," he says tightening his grip on me. "The cabin was confiscated by the authorities the last time."

"Then where?"

Jacob sighs noisily. "I have no idea." These words terrify me.

We have a quick breakfast at the hotel before heading out. While going over the first part of the plan several times, Jacob's hands never stop tapping the steering wheel. It's the first time I see how nervous he is. He's been calm and confident, but this part of the plan has him unsettled.

"She'll probably throw me out," he says.

Placing my hand on his leg, I say, "I don't think she will. She's your mother, and mothers who haven't seen their sons for seven years don't throw them out."

Although unspoken, I'm almost sure what Jacob is thinking. Most sons don't send their brothers and father to prison. She might very well kick us out, she certainly has enough reason, but I don't think so.

Pulling into Abuela's parking lot, Jacob says, "I'm trying to think of a way that I can keep my mother out of this." He runs his hands through his hair, making it stand on end. I reach over and smooth his curls back down. "This is the best way."

"It is."

Jacob pulls me into his arms and kisses me slowly, as if he's saying goodbye. Please, God. I walk in first, and when Jacob follows me, a loud gasp comes from behind the counter.

"Emilio?" his mother says. Jacob nods, and she rushes from behind the counter. To my shock she starts pummeling him in the chest speaking rapid Spanish. Then she breaks into tears and collapses against his chest, sobbing and saying, "Mijo" over and over. Jacob murmurs to her in Spanish.

She leans back and takes his face in both her hands. "I'm sorry, Mama," he says and kisses her cheek, which starts another round of sobs.

A small crowd of people appear from the kitchen, their mouths open in surprise. Not all of them look happy to see my husband. A woman around the age of Jacob's mother approaches and gently leads the two of them to a small booth in the corner. I follow awkwardly behind them. Jacob slides in the booth to sit beside his mother. I hesitate at first but then ease myself across from them.

Mrs. Vasquez doesn't take her eyes off Jacob as she dabs at her face with a napkin. "Mama," Jacob says. "This is my wife, Katherine."

Her eyes widen, "Esposa?"

"Yes, Mama. Please speak English," he says. "Katherine, this is my mother, Maria Vasquez."

I smile despite my nervousness. "It's so nice to see you, Mrs. Vasquez." I'm pretty sure she won't remember me from before, but just in case, I didn't want to pretend that this was the first time we've met. She nods to me without making eye contact.

"You must be hungry," she says, nudging Jacob to let her out. As she stands, she touches his face again and says, "Emilio."

After she disappears into the kitchen, I ask, "What was she saying?"

He smiled. "Not much. Just scolding me for not contacting her. I apologized and told her that I couldn't, and she scolded me some more."

"I don't think she's too happy about you being married."

Giving me a sympathetic look, "Sorry about that. In her eyes, I'm still married to Gabriella. I'm pretty sure Gabby's married to someone else now though."

Mrs. Vasquez reappears with chips and salsa, followed by three other people bringing plates of food. It looks like enough to feed ten people. "I didn't know what you would like, so…"

A young man helping to bring the food, who looks to be about sixteen or seventeen, can't hide his contempt for Jacob. I study him, and he sharply turns his head toward me. Our eyes lock for longer than is comfortable, but I don't look away. After they place the food on the table, the boy is the first one to leave. He's probably on his way to alert EJ and Juan about Jacob's presence, which is what we'd expected.

They will come for us, that much I know. I'm just not sure if they'll approach us inside the restaurant or in the parking lot. Dread churns in my stomach. I force myself to eat a little though, both because I don't want to be rude, and I'm not sure when I'll eat again.

As we are finishing our meal, Jacob's voice drops to just above a whisper. "Mama, I have to warn you that I have to confront my brothers once again."

She gasps. "Oh, why can't my boys make peace? For me, Mijo, make peace, for me."

Jacob grabs her hand. "You know that's not possible. Not now. Not after…"

Her forehead wrinkles with worry, "Please, Emilio. I can't lose you again."

Using his free hand, he wipes her tears with a napkin. "I'm sorry, Mama. It has to be." She buries her face in her hands and sobs. "I love you. You know that. I don't want to hurt you any more than I already have. But they've threatened Katherine. She's my family now, and I have to protect her."

Mrs. Vasquez looks up at Jacob. I'm not sure if her look is fury or fear. "Will I never see you again?"

Pulling her against his chest, a single tear falls down his face. "I'm sorry, Mama."

As we cross the parking lot, Juan and Jimmy are leaning against the SUV. I instinctively reach for my gun and then remember that we'd purposefully left them locked in the vehicle. "You finally brought your lady to meet

Mama?"

Jacob pulls me into a tight hug and whispers in my ear, "I'm sorry, Katie."

Sorry? What's he sorry about? Jacob presses the keys to the SUV into my hand and says, "I love you." Realization hits like a sledgehammer to my stomach. "Leave her out of it," he says, "and I'll go with you peacefully," Jacob says.

Head reeling, it's as if everything is happening in slow motion. Jacob turns away from me, and it feels as if we are being pulled apart—like Velcro—it's almost audible. We were supposed to stay together. Jacob promised. Didn't he? "Jacob," I say, my voice barely above a whisper. He steps toward his brother, and I grab his arm. "Jacob," this time more forceful.

His eyes don't leave mine as he pries my hand away. "It has to be this way." As he steps out of my reach, Jimmy grabs Jacob's arms and holds them behind his back. Jacob doesn't even struggle. Juan steps forward casually at first and then practically runs to meet Jacob. I close my eyes tight, but I can still hear the impact of Juan's fist in my husband's stomach.

This isn't right. I'm supposed to keep him from dying, and I can't do that if they take him. "No!" I scream, clawing at Jimmy to get him to release his grip.

Breathing heavy, Jacob says, "Jimmy, make sure she doesn't follow." Jimmy releases Jacob and grabs my arm. I try to pull away, but his grip tightens, and I cry out in pain. "But, if you hurt her, Jimmy, I will kill you."

"You can't kill me if your dead," Jimmy says smirking.

Jimmy puts his arm across my shoulder, holding me tight. When I trap his hand with both of mine, Jacob shakes his head at me. Something about the look in his eye tells me that if I make a sudden move trying to twist away, he will pay dearly for my actions. I cover my mouth with my hands instead. A dark sedan with tinted windows pulls up right next to Jacob. He starts to climb in but hesitates. "You can't kill me until you get what you need from me, and you won't get that until I know she's safe. Then you can do whatever you want to me."

I watch in horror as the car disappears around the corner. *Please, God!*

We were supposed to be in this together. I never doubted that fact. Why do I keep trusting Jacob? *I'm never going to see him again keeps running around in my head.* How could he do this to me? But then another thought intrudes: *Jacob sacrificed himself for you because he loves you.*

And I hate him for it.

I try to pull my arm free, but Jimmy jerks me backward.
"Give me the keys, and I'll let you walk with me to the
office." I drop the keys into his hand, but before he
releases his grip, he says, "No running."

My face feels red hot from fury more than fear, but I
don't look away. Glaring, I say, "Where would I go?"

Releasing my arm, Jimmy smiles and gestures for me
to walk ahead of him. I can't help wondering if Mrs.
Vasquez has any idea what's happening to her youngest
son—if that's why she was so upset to say goodbye to
Jacob. What must it be like to have married into such a

family, to have your own sons destroy each other? I should feel sorry for her, but right now, all I can muster is anger at her for letting them grow up this way. Then realization hits: I married into this same family. Don't think about that right now.

Jimmy sits behind the desk this time, and I sit in the same chair I did last time. Jimmy pulls a bottle of whiskey and two small glasses out of the bottom desk drawer. He pours about two fingers into both glasses and slides one toward me. I ignore it at first, but then pick it up and drink it all in one go. Big mistake. Coughing, gasping, and crying, I can't even take in a breath. It seems to burn from my nose to my toes. Shielding my face with both hands I look toward the floor, trying my best to intake oxygen.

Jimmy chuckles. "Not a whiskey drinker, huh?"

I don't respond. Jimmy reaches behind him to a small refrigerator on the bottom shelf of the bookcase. He pulls a bottle of water out and tosses it to me. It bounces off the back of my arm and hits the desk, but I manage to catch it before it hits the floor. I drink it almost as fast as I did the whiskey.

What's happening to Jacob? Remembering his broken body lying on the floor in my home a couple weeks ago, I imagine all kinds of horrible things they could be doing to him. He hasn't had time to totally heal from that beating. After seeing all those photos of the Vasquez family's handywork, I don't have to use my imagination too much. One thing is for sure, they know how to inflict pain and how to prolong it.

"You know he brought this on himself," Jimmy says.

I narrow my eyes at him. "Shut up."

He stares at me for a minute before continuing. "I'm just saying. He betrayed the family. Enrique ain't never getting out. Somethin' like that can't be forgotten." He leans forward to emphasize his next words. "Or forgiven."

"Shut. Up." I'm surprised at how easily those words leave my lips. I don't think I've ever spoken them to a person before. Thought about it? Yes. But actually saying it? Never.

But that was pre-Katherine. The Katherine before the invasion, before Victor, and before Emilio. Post Katherine is not as careful as she used to be, both in her words or her actions. I'm not sure which Katherine I prefer. Pre-Katherine was innocent and pure. And weak. Post-Katherine is strong and refuses to ever be a victim again, so, for better or worse, post-Katherine is who I need to be.

Jimmy smiles and shakes his head. After pouring himself more whiskey, he raises the bottle to me. I take it as an offering and nod. I drink this glass in small sips. How can anyone think this stuff tastes good? It does work fast, I'll give it that, which is probably why I can't resist baiting Jimmy.

"So, why do you get the babysitting job, Jimmy? You draw the short straw or are you just the most dispensable?"

His lips raise slightly, almost like he's snarling, but then his expression returns to neutral. But I know I've hit a nerve, so I keep poking.

"Bet you wish you could be in on all the fun they're having with my husband—wish you could have a go, don't you?"

Balling his hands into fists, he says, "I'll get my chance. Don't you worry."

"You sure, Jimmy?" I say. His expression looks as if he wants nothing more than to jump over the desk and pummel me. Part of me wishes he would. Then maybe I wouldn't be thinking about what's happening to Jacob.

I let the silence sit for a few minutes—let him think about what I said. I study his face. He's not as handsome as Jacob or Juan, but he's attractive. Dark hair and eyes, a nose that's probably been broken at least once, and a wide mouth with big teeth, heavily muscled and tall, he's more brawn than brain. At least, that's my impression. He could snap me like a toothpick, but I risk prodding him further.

"Hey, where'd you get that scar?" I say gesturing to the deep white crevice that runs up his forearm. It looks as if whatever caused it took half the muscle along with it.

He jerks his arm back and lowers it behind the desk and out of sight. "I think it's best if you just be quiet now."

"Jacob do that to you? I mean Emilio. Did he do that?"

Jimmy winces. That's a yes. "You best shut your mouth, or I'll shut it for you."

I lean forward, placing both hands on the edge of the desk. "You can't hurt me. You know what my husband said he'd do to you if you did."

"Emilio ain't here right now."

I can see the war going on behind his eyes. He wants to hurt me, but he knows he can't. Or he shouldn't, at least. Not until Jacob gives them what they want.

"What do you get out of this? Do you get a percentage of what they make, or will they leave you out of that too?"

Jimmy slams his fist down hard on the desk, and I nearly fall out of my chair. I guess it's time to shut up.

Looking in every direction except at me, Jimmy drinks another couple of glasses of whiskey—mine's still half full. He's regained control of himself, his expression back to casual irritation. After about an hour, Jimmy tosses my keys on the desk in front of me. "It's best if you head straight back to West Virginia."

I snatch the keys off the desk and hurry through the door. I attempt to slam the door behind me but hit Jimmy with it instead. He curses. I smile.

Jimmy doesn't even try to hide the fact that he's following me. He rides my bumper and switches lanes every time I do all the way through Jacksonville. I drive straight through to Savannah and stop at the same hotel Jacob and I had the night before. I pop the hatch to get my bags and notice Jacob's sitting next to mine. The sight weighs my heart down even more. Please, God.

As I turn to go into the hotel, Jimmy waves at me from the cab of his truck. He'd be there watching all night. I wonder if he'll be gone in the morning or if he's planning to follow me all the way to West Virginia.

But I'm not going back to West Virginia. I'm going back for Jacob.

I'd paced the room for hours, trying to figure out my next move. I couldn't drive Jacob's SUV back to Jacksonville. I had to get another car. In the movies, a person in my situation might steal one, but this isn't a movie, and I'm no thief. At 3:00 a.m. I'm ready to go. Peeking through the curtains, I see Jimmy still parked out front. But that's okay. I'd instructed the Uber driver to pick me up behind the hotel.

Now, as I drive my rented Camry back to Jacksonville, all I can think about is what's happening to Jacob and how I can possibly save him. How is 125-pound me supposed to get Jacob safely away from his brothers who are hell bent on exacting vengeance on him? The more I think about it, the more I'm convinced that it'll be impossible. But, I have to try.

You can do this. You can do this. You can do this. You WILL do this.

I have to start with the plan—the one that I thought we had before Jacob betrayed me. Again. I know that he was only trying to protect me, but I can't get over the deception. How long had he been planning to keep me out? We'd agreed that he needed me for his plan to work. If I think about it, the only person he really needs is Agent Stuart. Where is Stuart right now anyway? He probably knew Jacob was planning to leave mislead me. This thought allows me to refocus my fury on the agent. He should've warned me

Jacob had to know that even if he left me in Charleston, I would've followed him. The best way to keep me safe was to keep me with him as long as possible. Does he actually think that I won't try to find him now? He still sees me as the old Katherine—the one who would never attempt anything so risky—the one who runs. I'm not her anymore. I can't be. Even if I fail, I have to be the kind of person who would risk everything to save the one I love. If Jacob gets himself killed before I find him, I'll never forgive him.

I'll never forgive me.

I park down the street from Abuela's. I flop down the visor, so I can get a look at myself in the mirror. Running my fingers through my hair, I debate whether to put on the black ball cap that's currently sitting on the passenger's seat. I'd bought it, along with the black jeans, t-shirt, and hoodie, at a twenty-four-hour Walmart while I waited for the rental company to open. I'm not sure why. It just seemed to be the proper attire for sneaking into the Vasquez secret lair, wherever that is.

I adjust my oversize hoodie to make sure my gun's bulk won't be noticeable. For the third time, I'm marching right into the enemy's camp, this time fully understanding the danger I'm entering. I can't let myself react to my fear. I welcome it as fuel to get me through the next several hours. I have to find Jacob. Failure is not an option. But in order to succeed, I'm going to have to do uncomfortable things. The first of which is just beyond Abuela's front door. If Jimmy hasn't figured out that I'm not in the hotel by now, he will as soon as I enter the restaurant.

A young lady greets me. "I'm sorry, but we don't open for another thirty minutes."

"I need to speak with Maria Vasquez." I speak sharply. For a moment, I wonder if I should use a gentler tactic. Then I remember who has my husband, and I know this is no time to be polite. However, my demeanor seems to have temporarily paralyzed the girl. "Please," I add firmly, and she disappears into the kitchen.

Maria Vasquez is accompanied by the same woman Jacob left her with yesterday. I consider asking to speak with her alone, but the tension that has been building since Jacob disappeared won't allow it. "They have him," I say. "Emilio. But you knew that already, didn't you?"

She shakes her head and says, "I did not know."

I narrow my eyes, not even trying to be subtle in my scrutiny. "Don't try to deny it. You can't be in this family as long as you have and be oblivious."

"No, no, no," she says shaking her head as if by her saying the words and making the movement will make them true. She's trembling. The other woman guides her to a chair, murmuring in Spanish.

"I need to know where he is."

The other woman places her hands firmly on her waist. "She does not know, she told you that. Can't you see you're upsetting her?"

I can see it, and I can feel it, but I can't afford to give in to her pain. Not now. I take a deep breath, drawing in strength. I stand tall. Firm. Although, I'm afraid that a strong wind would knock me off my feet. "She should be upset," I say. Turning toward Mrs. Vasquez, "You know what they're doing to him. To Emilio. To your son," the word your thick with accusation. She winces, covers her face with her hands and begins to sob. Empathy threatens me to back down, but I can't give in. Not this time. "You know what they did to Antonio."

The other woman takes in a sharp breath. "You don't know what you're talking about. Leave. Now."

I take a step forward. "I do know. I saw the pictures."

She balls her fists at her side. "Emilio killed Antonio."

"No. He didn't. You know that, don't you Mrs. Vasquez?" I say glancing at her.

"Emilio killed his own cousin. He betrayed his family," the woman says.

Over the woman's shoulder, I see a group of people huddled together in the doorway to the kitchen, but I don't look their way. My eyes are locked with this woman.

Jacob's mother raises her face to look at the woman. "Camila, Emilio did nothing to Antonio."

"He loved Antonio," I say. I'd say like a brother, but in this family, it doesn't really fit. "Why do you think he turned on his own brothers? He did it to avenge Antonio."

"You are mistaken," Camila says. "Family does not turn on

family."

"Tell that to Antonio," I say. I squat in front of
Jacob's mother. This time, my tone is gentle when I say,
"Please, Mrs. Vasquez. For J—for Emilio. You must know
somewhere they might take him." She shakes her head. "It
may be too late," I say, "but I have to try to help him."

She looks at me, eyes stricken. "What can a little
woman do to save Emilio against so many?"

I take her hand. "I'm tougher than I look," I lie. "I
love your son, Mrs. Vasquez. I have to try, no matter what
it costs me. Please."

Mrs. Vasquez speaks quickly to Camila in Spanish.
The two women stare at each other. "Camila, this has
nothing to do with you." Camila returns to the kitchen
taking the onlookers with her. Mrs. Vasquez folds her
hands and rests her forehead against them and closes her
eyes. She must have come to a decision because when she
opens them, she stands and says, "Wait here."

She returns a few minutes later. "I have spoken with
EJ, and he says that they do not have Emilio. He says he
hasn't seen him in years." Stepping forward, she grabs my
hand firmly as if she is shaking it, but instead she presses a
folded piece of paper into my hand. She holds my hand
with both of hers, an expression of desperation on her
face. "Perhaps it's best if you return to West Virginia."

"Perhaps it is," I whisper, "But, I'm not leaving here
without my husband."

She nods, and I rush out of the restaurant. I turn the

opposite way from my car and walk a couple blocks before turning down a side street. I glance behind me a few times. Mostly, I look in the windows of the shops to see if I can see the reflection of someone following me. I don't see anyone, but just in case, I step into a small restaurant and ask to use the bathroom. I find a door that leads to the alley, step outside, and start running.

The paper seems to be burning a hole in my hand, but when I return to the car, I don't open it. I just start driving. I use the same defensive techniques driving as I did walking to make sure I'm not being followed. After about fifteen minutes, I pull into a convenience store parking lot. I unfold the paper to find a crudely drawn map with the words Hadley Farm at the top. I consider calling Agent Stuart with this information, but I have no idea how I would describe where I'm heading. Maybe I'll text him once I find it. Although Jacob probably already knew he would be taken there, despite telling me he didn't know where, so Stuart should already know the location.

It takes me several minutes before I know which way I should drive, and I lose track of how many times I have to stop to reconsider the map. Once I figure out the top of the map pointed west instead of north it goes easier. Nearly two hours later, I find the Hadley Farm sign at the beginning of a long driveway. I can barely make out the metal barn at the other end.

My heart is in my throat. Jacob is in there, and he needs me.

After driving past the property a few times, I find a place to park my car behind some trees just off the main road. Hadley Farm isn't a farm at all—just one large metal building surrounded by enormous trees that block the view of the building almost completely. If I hadn't been looking for the place, I would've missed it altogether.

After pulling my hair into a tight ponytail, I grab the ball cap and put it on, making sure the brim is low enough to hide my face. I'm not sure why. If I'm seen creeping up to the building, it won't matter if the Vasquezes recognize me. They'll probably shoot first and ask questions later. It's too warm for a hoodie, but I don't want to leave it behind just in case. Doors locked, purse in trunk, keys in pocket, and both guns securely fastened to my body, I step into the trees.

After about a half hour of walking I start to think that I'm somehow moving in the wrong direction. I'm either farther from the building than I'd thought, or I'm lost. With each step, panic pushes my heart to my throat. I want to cry. I want to curl up in a ball, lean against a tree, and bawl. This is all too much. I'm so close to Jacob, but even if I manage to make my way in the correct direction through these trees and find the building, I have no idea what I'll do once I get there. I've been afraid for Jacob, but now, I'm afraid for myself. What will they do to me?

I stop walking. Leaning against a tree, I take deep breaths to try and slow my heartrate. Breathing deep, I hold my breath as long as I can before blowing it out in a rush, and with the breath, I release enough of the tension to be able to keep going.

I'm sweating profusely. Damn, Florida is hot, even in the shade. Too hot for this stupid hoodie. I consider taking it off and tying it around my waist, but that would hinder access to my gun. But, if I faint from heat exhaustion, my gun won't do me any good anyway.

The clearing that houses the metal building appears abruptly. I try to remain concealed within the tree line while I figure out what to do next.

There aren't any vehicles parked in front of the building. It looks vacant; however, if I concentrate, I can hear men's voices. There are two sets of double doors in the front of the building large enough to admit a large tractor or other farm equipment. I move along the tree line to get a look at the side of the building.

There's a regular size door and a couple large open windows. I have no idea how I'm going to make it across this clearing and to the side door undetected. And even if I risk it, I might only find a locked door. I crouch behind some trees that are about twenty to thirty feet from the door. It might as well be a mile.

I close my eyes, mustering courage to move forward. Please, God. Before I get a chance to step out, a gray pickup truck turns onto the drive going way too fast. It stops abruptly in a cloud of dirt and loose gravel. Jimmy leaps from the truck and runs inside the side door. It's not locked.

Jimmy is greeted with shouts and curses. Using the distraction to my advantage, I run crouched over to avoid being seen through the windows. Easing the door open, I step into a small office. This one is not nearly as elaborate as the one above Abuela's, but even in its simplicity, there's something terrifying about it. Maybe it's because I know what happens in this building. There's no one for miles, so any screaming that might come from those being tortured wouldn't be noticed.

The shouting hasn't let up—Jimmy giving as much as he's getting as he defends himself. He'd watched the door all night and all morning and never saw me leave. Evidently, that was no excuse for letting me outsmart him.

Creeping to the door, I hold my breath as I peer through. A large backhoe and three pickup trucks block my view from the commotion. My mind tries to imagine what that backhoe could be used for, but I press the thought down deep. Later. I can speculate later.

It's now or never. I move as quickly and quietly as I can to hide behind the truck nearest the office door. I listen for a few minutes as Jimmy makes excuses for my escape. "She's not the timid housewife we'd expected. Didn't even have the sense to be scared. I'm telling you, she didn't even blink."

I risk a glance over the truck. Jacob is tied to a chair in the middle of the room. His eyes are swollen almost shut, and dried blood streaks from below his nose, covering his mouth and chin. Slightly hunched, Jacob's face is turned to the side, watching. The men are so engrossed in their conversation and secure of their location that they don't see me as I take aim with my 9mm.

One of them glances at my husband. Jacob grins, and the man backhands him so hard that it tips Jacob's chair onto its side. The man leans in with his face inches from Jacob, and I pull the trigger.

The water bottle on the table next to the arguing men explodes. Chaos ensues as the men try to determine what just happened. The man bent over Jacob straightens and reaches for the empty shoulder holster he's wearing.

"Step away from my husband," I say.

He narrows his eyes. "You must be the Mrs."

"Get away from him," I say.

"You and I both know you're not going to shoot me."

"Funny. Victor said the same thing just before I killed him." His eyes widen. He'd obviously not known that I was the one who shot Victor. Jacob shoots a warning look at me, but I continue. "Set his chair back up and untie him."

The man lifts Jacob's chair up. I have their attention, but now what? I hadn't thought this through. Am I really expecting them to just hand Jacob over, let us leave, and we'll all live happily ever after? I should've talked to Agent Stuart before I did anything. What was I thinking? "Untie him," I say.

I glance at Jacob, and his terrified expression stops me cold. Cold metal presses against my temple. "Now, Katherine," Juan says, taking the gun out of my hand. "You don't want to get yourself hurt, do you?"

How many times had Jacob warned me to always be aware of my surroundings? "Watch your 360," he would say. I'd been so focused on my husband's condition; I hadn't noticed Juan. There's nothing I can do about it now except submit. Possibilities of what might happen to us try to peck their way into my brain, demanding my attention. It takes effort to bat them away.

Juan leads me around the truck to a chair that had been pulled away from behind the table. He pats me down, I was hoping he wouldn't, and finds my 42. His eyebrows raise as he inspects the teal gun, and he smiles at me. "Sit."

The chair is wet from the water bottle I killed, but I sit anyway.

"How the hell did you get out of that hotel?" Jimmy yells.

"Shut up, Jimmy," Juan says. Stroking his beard as if considering, he says, "We were just discussing with Emilio how he's going to finish what he started for us before we were rudely interrupted." I assume he means Jimmy's interruption, not mine. "But now, what are we going to do with you?"

I stare at him for several seconds. "He can't do anything with his hands tied behind his back."

The corners of his mouth raise a little. "Suppose you're right," he says. "Jimmy."

Jimmy's mouth drops open for a second, and then he moves to untie Jacob's hands. Jacob rolls his shoulders to loosen them and then winces, and that's when I notice them.

Both of his thumbs have been dislocated.

We lock eyes for a moment before Jacob says, "I told you, I need to get something to finish."

"And I told you, dear brother," Juan says, "that you aren't leaving here." He doesn't say the rest, but he doesn't have to. He's not planning on either one of us leaving here. Ever.

"Then send her," Jacob says nodding his head toward me.

Juan smiles wide. "Do you think I'm an idiot?"

"I'll come right back," I say. "You have my husband."

"You and what army?"

I stare at him trying my best to show the right amount of fear—enough that would convince him that I wouldn't risk Jacob by bringing the authorities. Juan lifts the gun and points it at Jacob. "How about I just shoot you unless you get this thing done now."

"Go ahead," Jacob says. "Either way, you won't get what you need unless I have that zip drive."

"Or her," Juan says pointing the gun at me. Jacob jumps to his feet, and about five guns appear pointing at him.

"That's enough," a man said coming from the shadows. "No one kills Emilio except me, and that ain't happening until he's done." Looking at Jacob, "You sure you need that drive?"

Jacob nods.

"Lower the guns!" he shouts, and the guns disappear. "Can't you just tell us where to find it?"

"It has to be either me or Katherine," Jacob says. "EJ, I'm not lying."

EJ shakes his head and rubs his beard.

"You could send the babysitter with me," I say. Jimmy flinches.

Smiling wide revealing the family dimples, EJ says,

"The babysitter. I like that." Still looking at me, he says, "Jimmy." Jimmy starts to protest, but EJ's stare silences him.

"Jacob," I say and take a step toward him. EJ blocks my way. The man is at least six three and a good two hundred-fifty pounds of muscle. His hair is graying at the temples and there are gray streaks in his goatee. His command of the room is not just because he is the oldest Vasquez brother. He has an air about him that would make anyone take a step back in his presence.

I look around the big man, and lock eyes with Jacob. His face is even more swollen than it was when I found him on the floor of our house, and he looks so tired. Has he slept at all since yesterday? His forehead is tight with worry as I'm sure mine is. "You know what to do, Katie."

I do know. At least I know where to begin: the safety deposit box at Ameris Bank. I need to contact Agent Stuart but am not sure how I'll manage it with the babysitter's hovering. I have to. It's our only chance of making it out of all of this alive.

Jimmy approaches and reaches to grab my arm. "Don't touch me. I'll come with you. Just don't touch me." I lead the way out the door to Jimmy's truck.

"Sit down, little brother." EJ's tone doesn't match his words. I say a silent prayer that they won't hurt Jacob anymore while I'm gone. Please, God.

Jimmy and I stop at the Camry to get the business card and safety deposit box key out of my purse. I'd hoped that Jimmy would stay in the car while I rummaged through my purse, but he stood so close to me, I could feel his body heat and sense his stress. Finding the business card and key, I hand him the card. As he's looking at it, I slip my cellphone into my pocket. I pull out my wallet, remove my driver's license, and slide it into my back pocket.

After about five minutes of driving, Jimmy says, "Give me your phone."

I look at him and try to decide whether I should deny having a phone.

"I saw you put it in your pocket. Hand it over." I do. He watches me as he rolls down his window and throws my phone out. "What else do you have in them pockets?"

"Just my keys," I say. He snaps his fingers and opens his hand. I'd been hoping to be able to use them as a weapon against him, but I drop them in his hand.

"What else."

"Just my ID," I say showing it to him. I'll need it to get into the safety deposit box."

"What else?"

"Nothing else."

Jimmy slams on the brakes, stopping in the middle of the road. It's a good thing this road is so deserted. He'd wanted to shock me, to intimidate me into submission, and for a moment, it works. "What? Else?"

My eyes well up as I pull my grandmother's rosary out

of my pocket. My mind races to come up with ways I can keep from having to give it to him because one thing is for sure, I'm not giving this asshole my grandmother's rosary.

He stares at the white beads dangling from my hand. The menacing expression he wore before smooths out into something else. Reverence, perhaps. "You can keep that," he says softly and starts driving again.

Closing my hand around the rosary, I let my breath out slowly, and relief comes over me like warm water being poured from a pitcher onto my head and cascading down my body. I turn to look out the passenger side window, hoping that he can't see the tears falling. I allow myself a few minutes of release, but I can't let my guard down. Not now.

One more deep breath, and then I force myself to look out the windshield. No more hiding my face. I stare straight ahead and purposely remember everything that has happened in the last twenty four hours—meeting Jacob's mother, Jacob's capture, sitting in the office with Jimmy, the agony of driving away from Jacob to Savannah, confronting Mrs. Vasquez, finding Jacob, and seeing his battered face and dislocated thumbs. I hold the thought of Jacob's hands the longest. His hands that had always been gentle and loving to me are the same hands that had inflicted the same torture that he now endured. If he wasn't my husband, I may think that he deserves this. But he is my husband, and I can't bear to think about him broken. I have to get him out of this, but I'm not sure how. Once they have the zip drive, they'll kill him.

And then they'll kill me, and then bury us both somewhere in the woods. Fear reaches its hand out and grabs my throat, and my breathing speeds up. Get yourself together, Katherine. I can't give in to the fear. I have to stop them from killing Jacob. That's all that matters to me. All of this works to amp my emotions and turn them into tools of strength and determination.

Jimmy hasn't said a word since he took my keys and phone. He's getting too comfortable. Too confident. Breaking the silence, I say, "Are you always their errand boy?" His jaw tightens, but he doesn't answer. "That must be infuriating." I let my words linger so their meaning can sink in.

"I mean really, Jimmy, it must be quite tiresome."

His words escape through gritted teeth. "They trust me. That's all."

"They trust you," I say. "But only with babysitting and fetching things, not with important stuff."

Jimmy glances at me out of the corner of his eyes. "Keeping ahold of you is important."

"Perhaps," I say, "but not as important or as enjoyable as keeping ahold of my husband."

His hands tightly grip the steering wheel, turning his knuckles white and causing the muscles in his forearms to contract. "You should be quiet now."

I am for about five minutes. "What's that backhoe used for back there?" I almost don't catch the sudden widening of his eyes before his face returns to the not neutral but tense expression he'd been wearing since I started talking. "Are there bodies buried on Hadley Farm?" His reaction isn't subtle this time. His body jerks as if I'd just prodded him with a cattle prod.

"How many?" I ask lightly. Just trying to make everyday conversation. Jimmy doesn't answer. "Do any of them help you bury the bodies, or is that just your job?" This time his shoulders pull upward as they tighten. "Of course, it's just your job. Why would they do something so—so degrading when they've got you?"

"Shut the hell up!" Jimmy's voice bounces around the cab of the truck making me jump.

I shut up.

A meris Bank is almost empty of customers when we arrive. I show my ID to the man behind the counter and ask to get into box number 4620.

"Right this way," the man says. Jimmy tries to follow, but the man says that only the box owner is allowed in the viewing room.

"I'll be right outside the door," Jimmy says in a tone that warns me not to try anything stupid.

The man asks for my key and proceeds to retrieve my box. I consider telling him that I'm in trouble and that I need him to call the police, but that would put Jacob at further risk. I have to handle this myself. The box is placed on the table, and the man excuses himself.

Inside the box is a purple Glock 42, just like my teal one. I chuckle despite the flaming boulder of stress sitting just beneath my throat. I eject the magazine to find it fully loaded. A round is already in the chamber. I place the gun in my ankle holster and pray that I don't get frisked again.

I find the zip drive in the box as well as a cell phone with a note on it that says, "It's time," and below that, a phone number. I quickly turn the phone on, make sure it's on silent, and text the message from the note to the phone number.

There's a knock at the door. "Hurry up," Jimmy says.

I don't want to leave the phone behind. I'm 90 percent sure that the number I'd just texted was for Agent Stuart. If it was, maybe he'll be able to track me with the phone's GPS. I slide the phone into my bra under my left arm and once again worry about one of the Vasquezes finding it.

I don't struggle as Jimmy grabs my arm and not so gently leads me to the truck. He's not going to risk me escaping again. Before we get back into the truck, Jimmy makes me empty my pockets. I show him the zip drive, my rosary, and my ID. He takes the drive, and practically throws me in the truck.

I'm rubbing my arm where he'd been gripping it when he starts the truck. "Don't talk to me," he says. "I mean it. Don't say a word." His whole demeanor has changed. His dark eyes seem darker and somehow, deeper and hollower. His muscles are taut like an animal about to pounce—as if it's taking every bit of self-control to keep from attacking me. I don't know if it's the stress of having me out of his sight for those few minutes or if he'd talked to one of the Vasquezes while I was in the viewing room, but whatever it is, I take it as a warning not to harass him on the way back to Hadley Farm.

The phone vibrates, causing my whole insides to vibrate. Jimmy holds his hand out. "Give it." I consider pretending that I don't know what he's talking about, but I don't want to give him a reason to search me more fully. As I hand him the phone, Jimmy rolls down the window and tosses it out.

I turn and watch as my only hope of help from Stuart and the FBI bounces and shatters in the middle of the highway. I'm on my own, and the inevitability of Jacob's and my demise lands heavy in my stomach.

As soon as the truck is in park, I exit the vehicle and walk to the side door of the metal building. Jimmy jogs to catch up, grabs my forearm, and jerks me to a stop. He glares at me, causing me to shrink on the inside. On the outside, however, I don't break eye contact. Jimmy turns on his heel and walks to the door, pulling me behind him. I have to jog to keep up with his long strides.

Jimmy wordlessly hauls me up to Jacob and hands the zip drive to my husband. "Finish it, asshole."

Jacob curls his fingers over the drive and awkwardly attempts to insert it into the laptop on the table. The task is impossible without the use of his thumbs. I step forward and help him place the drive into the USB slot. Jimmy yanks me back almost pulling me off my feet.

Jacob stands and steps toward Jimmy. Jimmy has a couple inches on Jacob. "Watch it." The words grind out of my husband, and the look in his eyes is more frightening than I have ever seen him give. Jimmy winces, and I feel him tremble for a moment before regaining control of himself.

EJ's voice booms from across the room. "Back off, Jimmy!" His voice drops to an even yet menacing tone when he says, "Emilio, sit down."

Jacob holds his ground for a few seconds, letting Jimmy know that regardless of his dislocated thumbs and bruised body, he would break the man if he hurt me. Jimmy steps back without letting go of my arm.

Sitting on the edge of his chair, jaw tight, and whole body tensed, Jacob pounds away on the keyboard. EJ and Juan make their way over to stand behind him to watch the monitor. I notice that they don't stand too close. They allow enough room to be able to react if Jacob tries anything. The two men speak quietly to one another, brows furrowed, as if they're trying to determine whether the program is actually working. They nod, and I wonder how long it will take before they decide that Jacob's job is finished and it's safe to kill him.

I look around the room, weighing my options to delay them from acting. I'm not sure Agent Stuart has had enough time to assemble his team and get here. The silence in the room presses my stomach into my throat. The only sound is Jacob's occasional clicking. It takes every bit of self-control I have to keep from glancing toward the door.

I almost don't notice the sound coming from outside. At first, I think I'm the only one who had, but then I see EJ's expression shift from guarded anticipation of a large payoff to resolve that it was time to end this—to end Jacob.

Carefully turning my wrist upward so the front of it is facing toward Jimmy's thumb and forefinger, my eyes don't leave EJ. He shifts his weight as if he's about to make a move for his gun. I grab Jimmy's pinky with my free hand, hold it steady, and tear my other arm free from his grip. I felt the crunch of bone as everyone else in the room heard it.

Jimmy screams and unleashes all the fury toward me that he'd been holding in all day. "You bitch!" he yells as his backhand collides with my cheek. The force of the blow knocks me off my feet. Warm blood drips from the split in my cheek, and my eyes fill with tears from the pain. Somehow, I keep from crying out.

Several things happen at once. Jacob leaps to his feet. EJ pulls his gun. And I pull mine from the ankle holster, jump to a standing, and fire. EJ drops, and Jacob throws himself at me. I barely register the guns firing, men shouting, and the cannonball of fire that explodes in my shoulder before Jacob and I crash to the ground. My head bounces on the cement, and everything goes black.

As consciousness starts to return, it feels as if someone is trying to force a dull spear through my collar bone. I can almost see the bone splintering and tearing through muscle. Never have I felt this kind of pain—hot and sharp with bursts of excruciating. I move back and forth, trying to squirm away from the pressure. *What's happening?*

I peel my eyes open to find a man in black kneeling over me pressing a bandage against what I now realize is a gunshot wound. It almost seems separate from me at first; it's just too unbelievable to consider. In the next wave of agony, it comes together in my brain. I've been shot. And

Jacob...

Oh God, Jacob. My head jerks around trying to see beyond the man holding me down. I try desperately to sit up, but he holds me firmly. "Please, ma'am, you've lost a lot of blood."

"Jacob?" I say. His eyes narrow in confusion. "Jacob?" I say again, my voice rising as I frantically scan my surroundings for my husband. Then I spot his limp hand resting on the ground about six feet away. At least four people are hunched over his lifeless body. Is he dead? Oh please, he can't be dead. Please, God! He can't be dead.

"Jacob! Oh, God! Jacob!" I'm struggling as hard as I can to get up. My throat feels as if it's being filleted as I screech and scream and buck to get free. "Jacob!"

Two more men in suits drop beside me and do their best to keep me still. "Who the hell is Jacob?" one of them says.

"It's Emilio," someone says from beyond my sight. Agent Stuart's face comes into view. "He's alive, Katherine. It's bad," he says, "but he's alive."

"Why isn't he moving?" I scream.

"I need you to calm down, Katherine. Jacob will kill me if you bleed to death here." Stuart grabs my hand. "He's been hit several times, but he's still breathing. They're doing everything they can for him, but you need to let us take care of you," he says. "For Jacob."

The sirens grow louder, and I hope beyond all hope that they've arrived in time to save my husband.

Paramedics rush in to take over for the other men. One of them pushes his way to my side. "What've we got?"

"Not me," I say in a slightly calmer tone, "Take care of Jacob first."

Several other men carrying medical equipment hurry straight to Jacob. "He's in good hands," the paramedic says. He smiles, and I notice a slight dimple in his cheek. It's a nice dimple—not as nice as Jacob's—but nice enough. I sigh and lower my head back to the ground and wince as it touches. My head is pounding, my shoulder feels like it's exploding, and for the first time, I notice my left arm burning. Two gunshot wounds?

Jacob is life-flighted to the hospital and already in surgery when I arrive by ambulance. The doctor's concerned that my brain might be bleeding, so I have a CT scan before I'm cleared for surgery. I ask about Jacob before I allow them to put me under. "Still in surgery," the nurse says.

When I wake the first time, I'm told that Jacob's in ICU but stable. The next several times I manage to open my eyes, my vision is too blurry, and my brain is too foggy to make any sense of my surroundings. When I finally wake for real, I'm stunned to find Luke sitting beside my bed. Up to now, I'd managed to keep both sides of my life separate: the Harrison side, where my brother lives, and the side that put me in this bed, where my life with Jacob has led me. Conflicting emotions bombard me: immense relief to see him and total embarrassment that he now knows of my secret life.

Luke stands, "How are you feeling?" He looks as if he hasn't slept in days. Dark circles under his eyes, furrowed brow, and hair standing in every direction from his constant running his hands through it speak volumes about what the last several hours has been like for him.

I lift my head from my pillow and searing pain shoots through my left shoulder. "Like I've been shot."

He smiles weakly. "My sister—shot." He shakes his head. "And I thought I couldn't possibly be shocked anymore since—" He let the sentence fall away. "But this? Not in my wildest dreams."

"How did you get here?"

Luke chuckles. "I got this phone call from a strange man claiming to be your boss. He tells me matter-of-fact like, 'Your sister's been shot. The plane to Jacksonville leaves in three and a half hours. I suggest you be on it.' He says it like it happens every day." Running his hand through his hair. "I had to swallow all my questions, so I could make that flight. I was scared out of my wits."

"I'm sorry, Luke."

"I'm just glad you're okay," he says, eyes welling up.

"Where's Ed now?"

"He went to get something to eat in the cafeteria. He hasn't left your room since we got here."

"He's a good man," I say. "Do you know how Jacob is?"

Luke winces. "Last I heard, he's still stable." His jaw

tightens.

"How much did Ed tell you about all this?"

His eyebrows raise. "As little as possible," he says, shaking his head. "But enough to know that Jacob—" Luke closes his eyes for a few seconds, and when he opens them, he can't hide his anger. "Jacob's in trouble, and he's got you right in the middle of it."

"I put myself in it, Luke," I say. "Jacob tried to keep me out of it."

"You? This? This just doesn't seem like you."

"You're right," I say. "This is nothing like the me that you know. But the me that you know was lost when— when Mom died."

"He got you shot!"

Before I can counter, Agent Stuart walks in. "Look who's awake."

"Jacob?"

"Better. Still in ICU, but better."

"When can I see him?"

"Soon," Stuart says. I flash him my most intimidating glare. "Okay," he chuckles. "I'll check as soon as I leave here."

"Thank you."

"I'll need to take your full statement later, but give me the short version."

"Short version?"

He rolls his eyes. "How'd you end up shot?"

"Oh, that," I say in an attempt to stall long enough to decide how much to reveal in front of my brother. "I didn't think help was coming. Jimmy threw the phone out of the car, so I didn't see how." I shake my head. "EJ was about to kill Jacob, so I had to break Jimmy's finger and shoot EJ first. Then Jacob jumped in front of me and knocked me down."

"He took a couple more rounds than you did."

I don't even look in Luke's direction. "EJ?" I ask.

"Fine," Stuart says. "Your shot was a little to the right, so you only got his shoulder. His injury is a lot like yours, only on the right side."

"So, my body count is still one."

He nods. "Still one." Leaning his forearms on the tray beside my bed, he says. "We breeched the building as soon as we heard the first shot. Jimmy was already dead—shot by several different guns."

"Everyone else?"

"The only casualty was Jimmy."

My heart drops. Jimmy was a jerk, but of all of them, he was the most redeemable. "How did you find us?"

"The rosary."

"What?"

Stuart smiles. "After your solo trip to Jacksonville,

Jacob placed a tracking device in your rosary. He was pretty certain you'd have it with you."

That's how Jacob seemed to know where I'd been even though I never saw traces of him following. "When?"

"I don't know," Stuart says, "But that man always seems to intuit what might happen and prepare for it." He shakes his head. "What you did was—"

I interrupt. "Stupid? Reckless? Dangerous?"

"I was going to say fearless, but yours works too."

The room is silent for a good twenty seconds. "There are bodies buried on the property at Hadley Farm."

"How do you know?" Stuart says.

"Jimmy."

"He tell you that?"

"Not with words," I say.

Stuart shakes his head. "You know, you could have a future with the FBI if—"

"If I wasn't married to a felon?"

He smiles. "Something like that."

"If they find bodies on the property, will that be enough for Jacob to avoid prison?"

"It might," he says as he turns to leave. "But no promises."

"Stuart," I say. He looks back at me. "I didn't miss."

He smiles, shakes his head, and leaves.

Luke's voice is soft when he says, "Body count?"

I don't answer his question. I don't have to. "I'm more like Dad than either of us thought." Anyone can take a life in the right circumstances.

"No," Luke says. "I was thinking that you're a lot like Mom." My eyes widen. "She would've gone after us no matter what it cost her. Hell, she would've gone after Dad."

"That, she would." I close my eyes and have a difficult time opening them again. I'm just so tired. The sound of someone walking across the room makes me peel one eye open. Ed.

"What the hell were you thinking?"

"Are you asking as my lawyer or my boss?"

Ed crosses the room quickly, laughing and crying at the same time. He hugs me as carefully as he can manage. I don't tell him how much it hurts. I need this connection with my dear friend as much as he seems to. "You scared the living hell out of me."

"I'm sorry, Ed."

He shakes his head. "That man better appreciate all that you risked for him." He runs his hands over his bald head and says, "You did it. I never should've doubted your tenacity. You did it. You actually saved him."

I want to say that Jacob saved me too, but that will just start the familiar circular conversation about how I wouldn't have needed saving had it not been for Jacob, and

I would say that I put myself at risk and that he had tried to keep me out of it, and round and round it would go.

"I'll tell you all about it later. I can barely keep my eyes open."

"Oh, I know you need your rest. I'll take Luke back to the hotel for a bit. That's a good brother you got there."

The first time I see Jacob, he doesn't wake up. I sit next to him, hold his bandaged hand, and listen to the glorious sound of his breathing. There are tubes and wires everywhere; however, it appears he's breathing on his own, so that's a relief. I say as many of the prayers as I can remember from the night Jacob prayed the Rosary with me, which aren't many. Before I leave, I wrap my grandmother's rosary around his hand. There's no reason for him to keep track of where I am anymore. I'm not going anywhere without him. I kiss his cheek and whisper, "Thank you for not dying."

The next day as I round the corner going to Jacob's room, his mother is coming out. I step back to remain unseen and watch her leave. She has a fist full of tissues, and her face is blotchy from crying. I debate whether I should go to her but decide that there would be time enough for that later.

The head of Jacob's bed has been raised to a semi seated position. His eyes are closed, but I don't think he's actually sleeping. I creep up to the side of his bed. His eyes widen when he sees me, and a smile breaks over his face. The smile doesn't hide his pain, but its existence fills me with hope.

"I told you I wouldn't let you die," I say, and we both laugh and then wince. I know how badly it hurts me to laugh, I can't imagine how much it hurts Jacob. I cradle the side of his face with my good hand and press my forehead against his. "It's over," I whisper. "It's finally over."

Jacob drifts in and out of sleep while I sit next to him. I can't stop watching him breathe. During one of his alert times, I say, "I'm thinking about going back to church."

His eyebrows raise. "Really?"

I shrug. "It's probably time I stopped running."

"Where?"

I shrug again. "St. Mary's?"

"Really?"

"My mom was trying to return to her faith when she was killed. Maybe I should learn more about it."

Jacob squeezes my hand. "I think that's a great idea."

"I'm scared," I whisper. "Maybe I should wait until you get out of here, so you can go with me."

He's quiet for a few minutes. "I'm not coming home after this," he says. "I have to finish my last four years."

"But Stuart said that he could get you out of that."

"I know, Katie," Jacob says gently. "But there are consequences to my actions." He winks at me and tells me it was my influence on him that made him understand that. "Four years in prison isn't near what I deserve, but at least it's something." By finishing the four years left from his previous sentence, he'll avoid any time for whatever crimes he's committed over the past few months.

I feel my bottom lip quiver. "Four years?" It might as well be a lifetime.

"It will go quicker than you think." He reaches his hand out to cradle my face. "Don't wait for me to go back to church."

Shaking my head, "I don't think I can go alone."

"You, my dear Katie, are the bravest person I have ever known. Of course, you can."

Eleven. That's how many bodies they find on Hadley Farm. It's more than enough to put the Vasquez brothers away for the rest of their lives. It's still unknown whether Jacob and I will have to testify at a trial or if there will even be one. Either way, Jacob and I have no reason to be afraid of them anymore.

After spending a few weeks in the hospital, recovering from his injuries, Jacob is transferred to the Federal Correctional Institution in Morgantown, West Virginia. Ed helps him legally change his name. He'd asked me if he should change his name to Jacob Lewis, my mother's maiden name, instead of Jacob Varga. I'd given him such a hard time about stealing the name of someone's loved one. I told him that the original Jacob probably wasn't the only Jacob Varga and that, even if he was, he had used the name with honor. I can't imagine my husband going by any other name.

When his name was official, we got married again. To us, we'd been married all along, but it was important to be determined Mr. and Mrs. Varga legally. Yes, the preacher's daughter got married in a federal prison. Maybe when Jacob gets out, we'll get married in a church.

Agent Stuart has visited Jacob several times both at the hospital and at the prison under the pretense of asking Jacob's advice on a tricky case he's been working on. I think it's more to do with the fact that he really likes Jacob and values his friendship. Jacob told me that by helping the FBI, he might earn himself some time off his sentence. Whether he completes the whole four years or gets out of prison sooner, I'll be waiting for him.

I visit Jacob weekly. Who'd have thought that a girl who grew up as sheltered as I had, would end up visiting not just one family member in prison but two? One never knows.

As I sit at the table waiting for Jacob, I can't help but think about visiting my father We'd had a private room for both of those visits. I'm not sure how he'd arranged it, but I'm grateful that there were no witnesses to either meeting. The first one, I'd behaved badly; the second one was too intimate to be observed by outsiders.

I can't believe how many children are here. My first thought is that this is no place for kids. But would it be worse for them to never know their father? I guess an incarcerated dad is better than no dad. Right? I don't know. It just makes me sad for them. Across the room a small child chases his little sister around the table. The toddler's face is filled with joy, and even though it should seem out of place considering the setting, it doesn't. Have I ever felt that kind of unhindered joy?

Jacob is among the last inmates to enter the room. He walks stiffly as if in pain, and I pray that it's only because his body is still healing from his gunshot wounds and not because he's suffered something new. I roll my own shoulder a few times and still feel a sharp pain from mine; however, it still doesn't reassure me. Jacob's body has suffered way more than a thirty-four-year-old man's should.

We're allowed a hug and kiss, within reason, at the beginning and end of our visits. We're not allowed to hold hands. I cling to Jacob and bask in the warmth of him. He's thin—too thin. Someone clears his throat behind me, and I know that I have to let him go. "Are you okay?" I ask.

"Better now," he says with a wide grin. His freshly shaven cheeks allow his dimples to shine. Man, I love those dimples.

"You look sore."

Jacob doesn't answer at first. He narrows his eyes, plops his elbow on the table, and rests his chin in his hand, still grinning. "I'm sure you remember that I was shot recently."

Is he protecting me? Do I really want to know what goes on in here? "It's not from anything else?" He shakes his head. "Are you sure?"

"Positive," he says, but I'm not sure if I believe him. "Enough about me, how was your week?"

A piercing scream booms from across the room. The toddler that so joyfully ran around the room before is now squirming and crying, trying to wriggle out of what I assume to be her incarcerated father's arms. I don't know who I feel worse for, the child or the man.

"This is no place for kids," Jacob says, echoing my thoughts from earlier. But if we had kids while Jacob was in here, I'd probably bring them.

I tell Jacob about meeting my new niece at the hospital earlier in the week. "They named her Anna Katherine," I say with tears in my eyes. "I figured Luke would name the baby after my mother, but—"

Seeing Luke hold his baby girl made me wonder what

Jacob would look like one day holding our newborn son or daughter. He'll be a great father despite the one he had. I'm so happy for Luke and Lori, but I also ache for what can't be mine right now.

"That name is perfect." Jacob says.

I shrug. Changing the subject, I say, "I think I'm going to do it tomorrow."

"Really?" Jacob says. "Are you sure?"

"It's time," I say. "I think."

He smiles. "I wish I could go with you."

"Me too."

"You could wait."

A single tear escapes my eye and I wipe it swiftly away. "It's time."

"I'm proud of you," he says, and I know that he is. He's the only person in the world who understands.

The time passes quickly, as it always does during these visits. I do my best to memorize the feeling of Jacob's arms around me because I know that it will help me through the week.

The next day, I drive past St. Mary's twice before I finally have the courage to park. I can almost hear Jacob asking me if I was sure I want to do this. I'm not sure but get out of the car anyway.

I wonder what the reverend would say if he could see me now. I squeeze my hand around my grandmother's rosary, and a pang of loneliness washes over me. Loneliness for Jacob. Loneliness for my grandmother. Loneliness for my mother. I close my eyes and can almost feel her. As if the words are actually spoken, I hear my father saying, "Your mother would be so pleased." I don't even try to understand why he seems so much closer than my mother does.

Father Michael stands in the back of the church getting ready to walk down the aisle. His face lights up when he sees me. He reaches out, takes my hand, and beams. He holds my gaze for a moment before saying, "Welcome."

"Thank you," I say, blinking back tears. Welcome. I haven't felt welcome in a church since before my mother died—except for the middle of the night visit to this very church.

I slip past him and into the back pew. The church looks different in the daylight. As I take in the space, my eyes stop on the large crucifix hanging behind the alter. The sunlight shines through the windows and points right at it, like a spotlight from heaven. Suffering Jesus. I can almost hear my father say, "The Catholics got that right." I smile and nod. I forgive you, Dad. Maybe this time it will take.

I bring my hands to my mouth, both wrapped tightly around the rosary, and close my eyes. I'm just so grateful. I marvel at the irony of it all. How can I be grateful after all that has happened to Jacob and me? I'm scared and nervous and uncomfortable but so very grateful. After all that we've been through, after all that we've survived, and even though we can't be together right now, our puzzle is once again connected, and we are whole.

At least, as whole as we can be.

Maybe that's why our life's puzzle is made up of so many pieces. Each piece is forged from our experiences. From our joys and sorrows and pain. Some pieces we'd like to throw away, but we can't. We can't deny or ignore the fact that they exist, even if it cuts us to look at them. The ones we avoid, the ones we would like to forget, the ones that make us feel ashamed, mold and shape us just as much as the ones we love. Perhaps, they shape us more. All the broken pieces come together to make the whole.

Life is a puzzle. Every event, whether past, present, or future, has its place in the puzzle. No matter what the shape, its pieces fit together perfectly. At birth, my puzzle had few pieces. As I grew, so did my puzzle. It all fell apart for a while and rebuilding it about destroyed me. Looking at it now, I see every corner, every painful piece, and appreciate its beauty.

And I am grateful.

ACKNOWLEDGMENTS

There are so many people I need to thank for helping me with this book. First of all, I need to thank my husband and family for putting up with me in this process. Your patience is appreciated.

Thank you to my brother, Dean Reynoldson, for sharing his expertise on human trafficking and identity theft and to my friend, Joe Savilla, for your advice on police procedure. I apologize to you both for any straying from reality that may or may not have happened. This is fiction after all.

I'm grateful to my writing professors from Franciscan University of Steubenville, Dr. David Craig and Dr. Mary Antoinette Sunyoger, for always challenging me to do my best work, even when it hurts. I can't tell you how many times while trying to decide if a scene is good enough, I heard Dr. Craig's voice say, "I can't feel it."

Thank you to my mentor, Richard Paul Evans, and the Author Ready community. A special thanks goes to my writer's group. Tasha Howe, Sharon Leino, Deanne Taylor, and Mary Flint, words cannot express what your guidance, support, and friendship means to me. And that's saying something. I'm a writer.

ALSO FROM LISA R. PERRON

Fiction

Among the Reeds

I Am Cancer

Nonfiction

When God Said No

Find Lisa at www.lisarperron.com

 authorlisarperron

 lisarperron